Hard Times in the
HOLLOW

David Coleman

NFB
Buffalo, New York

NFB
<<<>>>
NFB Publishing/Amelia Press
119 Dorchester Road
Buffalo, New York 14213

For more information visit
Nfbpublishing.com

For the rest of my siblings; Chris, Mary, Tom, Dan and Ruth and the continuing story of my own my family.

Also by David Coleman

Rust Belt Redemption: A Tom Donovan Mystery
Two years ago Tom Donovan was a cop, working the rough and tumble streets of Buffalo's East side. One fateful night he was involved in the deaths of a Federal agent and an unarmed man

Shadow Boxing: Tom Donovan Returns
Buffalo New York Ex cop Tom Donovan is struggling with the events of his recent past, both physically and mentally, when an event from twenty two years ago captures his attention.

Souvenir: The Third Book in the Tom Donovan Series
Carolyn Krupp already has her hands full as a single mother raising a special needs child. When her brother Mark is assaulted and left for dead at the edge of a park she asks her neighbor, ex cop turned PI Tom Donovan, to look into the matter as the police seem to already have made up their minds that Mark was in the wrong place at the wrong time and Karma caught up with him.

Hard Times
in the Hollow

CHAPTER 1

February 1932

The still night air was bitter cold. The sound of the snow crunching under Jacob's boots seemed to amplify and echo off the trees as he made his way to the wooded blind where the shed was. They had selected a spot near the creek that separated his property from his father's.

When he entered the shed he cursed under his breath. The fires under the old milk cans that they used to cook the corn mash had almost died out. Where the hell was Willie? His brother was "simple" but he was a hard worker. Willie's biggest problem was that he was easily distracted and would lose track of time, especially if he was hunting. Jacob hung up the kerosene lantern and turned to grab some wood off the pile in the corner. He didn't hear Deputy Silas Ferguson enter the doorway.

"Jake," Ferguson said.

Jacob spun around and dropped the wood he was holding. "Damn it Silas!" he said, "You scared me half to death."

Ferguson took a step in. Jacob noticed he was holding a shotgun at his side. He stomped the snow off his boots and looked at Jacob. "Kinda sorry to run into you here."

Jacob could sense that something was wrong. His eyes swept the small shed, searching for an exit, and he saw only the logs at his feet. "What are you doing out her Silas?" he asked, trying not to sound confrontational.

"Afraid we got some bad news the other day," he said, never taking his eyes off Jacob. "The Treasury Department is opening an office in Jamestown. In a couple of weeks there are going to be prohibition agents running up and down the valley."

Jacob shook his head. "Wait a minute. What about our deal?"

"Deal?" Ferguson asked, a smile creeping across his lips.

"Yeah Silas, we pay you to take care of things like that."

Now Ferguson shook his head. "That was with the State Police," he responded. This is the Federal Government. We don't have that kind of pull."

"Silas, you know we need the money to keep the farm going, at least until we get back on our feet."

"Sorry Jake, It's been a good run but it's time to shut it down..." as Ferguson finished Jacob noticed he tightened his grip on the shotgun.

Jacob was desperate. Last year's corn and hay harvest had been thin. His father's effort to modernize the milk production had taken a disastrous turn, and there were mouths to feed and taxes to pay, "Don't forget you and your father have a lot to lose here too," he said.

Ferguson squinted and said, "How do you figure?"

"If the voters found out that you and your daddy were taking money from bootleggers to look the other way for the last few years, he might not have an easy time of it in the next election."

The shed fell deathly quiet. The only sound was the slow drip from the condenser into the collection tank. After a moment, Ferguson spoke, "Like I said, I'm sorry we had to bump into each other Jake."

Jacob took a step back but Ferguson had already leveled the shotgun at him.

"You son of a bitch..." was all Jacob got out. The shotgun roared and the double load hit Jacob square in the chest. He flew back into the wall and slid down it. His head was bowed onto his chest. His eyes were open but unfocused. Ferguson stepped over to him and drew a pistol off his belt. He cocked the hammer and shot Jacob in the head. As the smoke was clearing and the ringing in his ears ebbing, he looked down at Jacob and repeated, "Like I said...sorry Jake."

Ferguson opened a case of bottles of mash and spent the next few minutes breaking them against the walls of the shed. Then he took the butt of the shotgun and hammered it against the collection tank until it fell off of its stand and the top came off. Finally he retrieved Jacob's lantern and stepped outside. As soon as he had taken a few steps backward he threw the lantern back through the doorway. At first nothing happened, he wondered if he would have to go back in. Then a small orange light sprang up: within seconds the shed was fully engulfed in flames.

Ferguson stood back and admired his handiwork. When he was satisfied with what he had done he turned to go back down the trail. Had his eyes adjusted sooner from the firelight to the darkened night, he might have seen Jacob's thirteen year old son, Adam, watching in horror from the trees.

CHAPTER 2

D inners at his grandparent's house were never pleasant for Adam Avery. This one was especially torturous.

Adam's father, Jacob had just been laid to rest in a plot about twenty yards behind the two story farmhouse that been his father's boyhood home. The weather had warmed up slightly the past week, but it still took the workmen hours to dig a hole suitable enough for Jacob's casket. Now the family sat around the table in stilted conversation, picking at a ham that had been intended for Easter.

At Adam's mother's insistence an Episcopal minister from Little Valley had been invited to say a few words at the service. He had done his duty and excused himself that afternoon. Technically, the family belonged to the Methodist church in Napoli, but Iris had alienated the Rev. Bowman over the course of his first year as head of the congregation. Adam had overheard his grandmother on more than one occasion saying that more harm than good had been done in the name of the Lord.

His father's absence at the dinner table was palpable.

Even though Jacob had been jaded by the events of his life, he could at least put on a good show for his family's sake, and carry on polite if mundane conversation. The only words being said came in clipped off sentences, little of which registered with Adam.

During dinner he stole glances around the table at the family. Aunt Connie, speaking in hushed tones to his cousin, Billie. Connie's husband John, looking distracted and far off. Uncle Willie, his father's "slow" younger brother, eating like his life depended on it. His grandfather Leon, laboriously working on his dinner with his one good arm and stiffened mouth.

His eyes finally came to rest on Grandma Iris. She was looking back at him with a look that he couldn't make out. Was it pity or something else? She held his gaze with her bright gray eyes until he broke it off.

After dinner the women went to the kitchen to clean up and the men went to the parlor to sit by the fire. Leon used to smoke his pipe after dinner but since the stroke the talk proved too frustrating. Soon he just got drunker and surlier. Adam hated being around his grandfather when he got like this. Leon would rail on about how the farmers were being treated by the government and the unfairness of it all. Adam excused himself at the first opportunity, put his coat on and went outside.

The cold night air helped to expel the stifled feeling he'd had all day. The moon was out and a pale blue light illuminated the yard. He found himself wandering back to the family's burial plot.

A light snow had fallen over the yard covering the muddy boot prints of the workmen. The fresh mound of the grave seemed to have rejected the powder and stood out like a black scar in the cemetery. There were only three other markers, Leon's parents and a sister of Jacob's who had been stillborn. Only Jacob's grave seemed real to Adam.

He had no idea how long he had stood there, listening to the stillness of the night, but after a while the cold began to permeate his wool coat and he made his way back to the house. As he approached the back of the house and the kitchen door he noticed it was ajar, probably to cool the kitchen off. He could hear Iris speaking as he stepped to the door. She was scolding someone.

"What did you think was going to happen?" he heard her say.

Adam's mother, Maureen responded, but Adam couldn't make out what she said. He stepped closer to the door.

"Did you think you were going to run it?" Iris asked with an increasing edge to her voice.

"I don't know..." Maureen started.

Aunt Connie said something that Adam couldn't make out. Adam hoped that she was trying to smooth things out. His hopes were dashed because whatever she said didn't sit well with Maureen.

"We've done everything you asked and then some," Maureen said raising her voice. "Jacob died working for this family!"

"I know that!" Iris replied. "He was my son before you got a hold of him!"

"I've got half a mind to take Adam back to Buffalo," Maureen said. She was trying to be strong, but Adam could hear a quiver in her voice.

Iris let go a short laugh. "And do what? Go back to your old profession?"

Iris's words hung in the air and brought the conversation to a halt. Adam had heard enough, he was about to open the door into the kitchen when it burst open and his cousin Billie came out, hauling a pail of dirty water. She looked up into Adam's eyes, her own eyes were moist. She shook her head and bit her lip then went to the barn without speaking. Adam stepped onto the threshold. His mother spotted him, her face was flushed with anger and she tried to smile at him. She untied the apron she was wearing and said, "Good, you have your coat. It's time to go home."

It was a half mile between the two families homes and Maureen didn't speak for the first half of the trek. Adam knew she was holding it in for his benefit, but his curiosity got the better of him. "What did Grandma say?"

Maureen slowed down and then came to a complete stop and turned to him. Adam had grown quite a bit in the last year and now stood almost eye to eye with his mother.

"Grandpa Leon is selling our part of the farm," she said.

"What? Why?"

She looked down at the road and then back at her son.

"The government is buying the land. It's part of the relief effort."

"What about us? Can we stay in the house?"

"No, love. The house is part of the property."

Adam shook his head. Once again he felt the world crashing in on him. His mind was a jumble of protests and questions that he couldn't put into words.

Maureen seemed to sense his dismay and put a gloved hand on his cheek. "We'll have to move in with Iris and Leon, for the time being."

Adam was fighting back the tears. He remembered and wished for the life they had before they moved to this God forsaken place.

PART ONE

CHAPTER 3

September 1918

Jacob Avery had been growing restless on his parent's farm. When word spread in early '17 that the American Expeditionary force was recruiting to go to Europe and fight the Hun, he stole away one day and took a train to Buffalo to enlist. He left a letter to his parents, apologizing for leaving without telling them, but he knew that even though they wouldn't approve, it was what he had to do.

It took some time, but his idealism and naivety were ripped away by the horrors of modern warfare. The Americans arrived and took up positions along the lines and trenches of the Western Front. The initial anticipation of battle came complete with cold nights, inedible food and the threat of mustard gas looming over them.

In the spring of '18 the Germans mounted what would be a last desperate offensive against the Allied lines. The offensive was repelled in a coordinated effort by the now centralized command under the French General Ferdinand Foch. Then the counter offensive began. The AEF was tasked with proving it could be relied upon to fight alongside the battle hardened

French and British troops. Finally one day, after the French artillery ceased shelling the German positions around the village of Catigny at 6:45 AM, Jacob's unit went over the top of their trench and advanced.

The Germans, still reeling from the French barrage, offered sporadic yet deadly, resistance. As the Americans crossed a field outside of the village they were met by a hail of bullets from a German garrison hiding in a farm house. Jacob took cover, throwing himself prone on the ground and laid like that with the bullets whizzing over his head. Finally, after what seemed like an eternity two French machine gun units arrived and cut the farmhouse to pieces.

The sergeant's whistle sounded and Jacob got to his feet. Directly in front of him lay Corporal Higgins, on his back with a bullet hole in his throat. He was gasping for air as the blood gushed out of his neck and ran down into the trampled grass. They moved on towards the farmhouse.

"Avery! Tanner!" the sergeant bellowed. "Clear that house."

Jacob went around to the side of the house and with a nod to Tanner, kicked the door in and leveled his weapon. He hadn't taken more than a step inside when out of the shadows a shape came towards him and he felt a jab in his chest. At first it was like the sharpest pinch he had ever felt and then the pain exploded through his whole torso. He instinctively dropped his weapon and grabbed at the object. He found his hand on the hilt of a German bayonet held by a man, bleeding from his own head wound. They stood and stared at each other in shock until Private Tanner stepped up next to Jacob and shot the German in the chest.

Jacob collapsed to the ground and lay on his side. The muzzle flash and the deafening report of Tanner's rifle were slowly subsiding and he realized he was going into shock. The dead German lay not three feet away. Jacob looked at him and saw a man, probably aged beyond his years by the strains of a seemingly endless conflict and he understood; there was very little nobility in dying for your country.

^^^

He would have gone back to his unit, he knew it. Not for his country or the cause or any other high minded principle, but he would have gone back for his fellow soldiers. It came as a relief however, that by September of '18 rumors were swirling of the Germans losing the will to fight and inevitably surrendering. After nearly four months in the hospital and a bout with dysentery Jacob had lost twenty pounds and his taste for battle; he was ready to go home. He wasn't looking forward to returning to his parent's farm just yet, he could almost hear his father's voice telling him what a fool he'd been and see his mother's disapproving looks. Still, he was tired of the army, tired of France and tired of being told what to do.

He spent a week in Marseilles before he was assigned to a transport heading back to the States. The ship's hold was packed full of wounded and shell shocked soldiers headed home and the air was heavy. Jacob sought relief by going up top, despite the chill North wind. On the second day out of port he came across a Marine, sitting by himself on a crate with his shoulders hunched. The man was absent mindedly holding a letter in his hand staring off into nothing. Jacob passed the man without being noticed. At first he thought he should just let him be, but there was something in the man's body language that made him turn back. Jacob took out a pack of his ration cigarettes and flicked one out. He tapped the man on his shoulder and said, "You look like you could use a smoke."

Jacob had only seen the man in profile. He looked to be heavy set with a shock of unkempt red hair. Then the man turned towards Jacob and revealed the tell-tale scars that were left on his face from the blistering that meant the man had survived a mustard gas attack.

The red headed man looked at Jacob blankly for a moment as if he hadn't heard what he said. Finally he smiled wanly and shook his head. "Thanks," he said. "But I just about coughed up both of my lungs over the last few months."

Jacob made a concerted effort not to stare at the man's deeply scarred face. "Sorry," he said and then an awkward silence ensued. The man looked back at the letter he was holding and Jacob took that as a sign. "Well, have a good night," he said and started to turn away.

"You go ahead and have one though," the man said. "I miss the smell."

Jacob pulled a crate up from near one of the hatches

and sat down. He thought about lighting the smoke but didn't. After another extended silence he reached out his hand.

"Jake Avery, 28th Infantry."

"Timothy Doyle, 5th Marines." He shook Jacob's hand. "Everybody calls me Red."

Jacob glanced down at the letter and asked, "Bad news?"

Red let out a sigh and said, "It's from my sister back home in Buffalo. My dad passed away in June. The worst part is I just got the letter before we shipped out yesterday."

"That's rough... sorry to hear that."

They talked on into the evening. They swapped their experiences from the front. Red's unit had been dug in at Belleau Wood, repelling repeated advances from the Germans when his unit got gassed. He told Jacob how, despite his injuries, he was lucky. He watched four other Marines choke to death right in front of him. He laid in a hospital bed for weeks with a fever and bandages covering most of his face. Finally he was deemed healthy enough to go home.

He was worried about his sisters, 17 year old Maureen, and 15 year old Maggie. They had no other family in Buffalo to speak of except for Red and their late father.

The two men spent most of the next three days of the crossing together. Despite their different upbringings they seemed to share the same opinions on many things. This was especially evident what it came to discussing their experiences and thoughts on the war they had just left behind.

On the last night before they were to arrive in New

York, they were sitting in their usual spot on deck and after a long period of silence Red spoke up, "Did you ever wonder what it was all about?"

The moon was shining down on them and a gentle breeze was blowing from the South. Jacob, slightly confused, asked, "What was all about?"

"The war," Red answered.

"Do you mean what caused it?"

Red shook his head and thought for a moment. Then he said, "No, all of that was in the papers. I mean, what were we doing there? What was accomplished?"

Jacob knew the stock answer was to free Europe from the boot heel of the Kaiser, but he also knew that Red was talking about something more. "I don't know, Red. I suppose we did the right thing, but at what cost?"

"And for whom?" Red said and then fell silent again.

Red and Jacob decided to catch a train together from New York to Buffalo and then Jacob would catch the Lake Erie Limited to South Dayton. After a particularly heavy coughing fit had subsided Jacob asked Red, "You should come out to the farm with me; the fresh air would do you good."

Red managed a smile and said, "What would I do on a farm? I wouldn't know my ass from a turnip. Besides I've got two sisters to look after now."

It was late afternoon when the train pulled into the station on Exchange Street, too late for Jacob to make his connection so Red insisted he spend the night at his flat on Mackinaw

Street.

They walked the few blocks from the station in their uniforms
with their duffel bags over their shoulders, earning more than
a few curious looks. The curiosity turned to pity and revulsion
when the people they passed by saw Red's face.

Jacob could sense Red's unease as they climbed the
stairs to the second floor apartment.

He knew Red was excited to see his family but at the
same time extremely self-conscious about his appearance. Red
tried the door but found it locked so he rapped gently on it and
waited. The sound of heavy footsteps approached from inside
the apartment. Jacob sensed immediately that something was
off. The feeling was confirmed when the door opened, revealing
a heavyset man with a ruddy complexion who Red obviously
didn't know.

"Yeah?" the man said, looking at them suspiciously.

Red was just staring back at the man, speechless. Jacob
finally interceded. "Beg your pardon sir, but we're looking for
Maureen and Molly Doyle."

"Never heard of 'em," the fat man said and started to
shut the door.

Red stuck his arm out and it struck the door. The man's
face looked surprised and then angry.

"This is our apartment you fat bastard!" Red blurted
out.

The man tried to push the door shut but Red held firm.
Something about Red's demeanor seemed to be unnerving the

man, he went from angry to frightened and a drop of sweat rolled down his brow. "Red!" Jacob said, putting his hand on his friend's arm. Then he looked at the man and asked, "How long have you lived here?"

"Three weeks, for Christ's sake! I don't know who you're talking about."

Jacob had managed to pull Red back far enough that the man was able to shut the door. Red's breathing was a rasp and Jacob eased his grip on him. Red looked at Jacob with the same anger that he had been directing at the stranger. Then he seemed to realize that Jacob was trying to help. He caught his breath and said, "The landlord. Flanagan."

They went back down to the first floor and Red found Flanagan's door and pounded on it.

"Flanagan! Open up! It's Tim Doyle!"

"I know who it is!" came a hoarse voice from inside the apartment.

"Open this door or I'll kick it in!"

"You'd better not! The cops are already on the way!"

Red took a step back and looked like he might explode. Once again Jacob took his arm calmly and said quietly, "Ask him about your sisters."

Red nodded and then shouted through the door, "Where are Maureen and Molly?"

"Damned if I know," Flanagan shouted back.

Jacob tried to stop him but it was too late. Red un-leashed a kick that shattered the old wooden door by the knob and it smacked into Flanagan who was standing behind it. Red entered the room with Jacob practically on his back. Flannigan had retreated to the nearest wall. He looked terrified and pathetic, a frail old man in a dirty undershirt and trousers.

"Where are they?" Red shouted.

"I don't know," the old man sputtered.

"Did you evict them?"

"I had no choice. They hadn't paid rent in four months."' The old man was shaking.

"For God's sake," Red said half trying to free himself from Jacob's grasp. "Our father just passed and you tossed them out?"

"I needed the money! They hadn't heard from you in months. They thought you were dead too."

Red stopped struggling, deflated. He just looked at the withered old man in front of him.

"Red, we have to go," Jacob said. He pulled Red out of the apartment and into the fading evening light.

Out on the street, Red stood looking down at the ground. His lips were moving but no sound was coming from his mouth. Jacob put his hand on Red's shoulder and said. "Red, where would they go? You said you've no other family in town?"

Red looked up and shook his head. He looked up and down the street and then seemed to think of something. "The neighbors."

"Who?" Jacob asked.

"The Farrellys. They live on the third floor."

Jacob looked back warily at the building they had just left. "Do you think they're home?"

"Probably not. They're either at work or down at Mahar's"

Mahar's was a tavern located around the corner on Louisiana Street. Red and Jacob walked in and scanned the dimly lit room. The floor was covered with sawdust and the air was filled with smoke and the smell of stale beer. Red headed over to the bar. It took a moment as the barman looked at him skeptically before a look of recognition flickered across his face.

"Red!" he exclaimed. "Damnit lad it's good to see you!"

"Hello Peter," Red said accepting the other man's hand.

After introductions were made Red cut off the small talk and stated his business. Peter Mahar shook his head gravely and said that he hadn't heard that Red's sisters had been thrown out of their home. He also hadn't seen either of the Farrellys in a few days.

"Buy these two war heroes a drink!" a voice boomed from behind them. Red whirled around when he felt a hand slap him on the shoulder. He was raising his fist until he recognized the man who was behind them.

Jacob had turned to the man too. He was tall and heavy, with a wool suit that was straining to hold his girth. The man looked at Jacob and said, "Friend of Red's? Good to meet you. the name's Denny, Denny King." He reached into his pocket and pulled out a business card and held it out with his chubby fingers. Jacob took the card. It read, *Dennis L. King, Secretary, Grain Scoopers Local #4.*

"You boys looking for work now that you're home? I'm the man to see."

"Now's not the time for that Denny," Peter the barman said. "Red's looking for his sisters."

King's face fell and then he glanced sideways. Red picked up on his discomfort and said, "What? What is it Denny? Have you seen them?"

King couldn't seem to look at Red directly. He opened his mouth and started to stammer something inaudibly.

Red dropped his pack and seized King by the lapels. "Speak up! Have you seen Maureen and Molly?"

The big man was shaken and tried vainly to free himself from Red's grasp. "Yes! I saw Maureen the other night."

"Where? Tell me where or I'll split your fat head open!"

"At Esmeralda's." The words gurgled out of King's throat.

The color drained from Red's face and he let go of King. The bar had fallen silent and Jacob glanced around not knowing what was going on. "What about Molly?" Red said between clenched teeth.

"I don't know..." King said, straightening his jacket. "I only saw Maureen."

Red's blood was starting to rise again. He glared back at King and asked, "Did you..."

King shook his head emphatically. "No sir! I was only

there for a drink."

Jacob was looking at Red, hoping for an explanation.
Red looked back at him briefly and then at Peter Mahar. "Pete,
do you have someplace where I could store my gear?"

"Of course, there's a room upstairs. Just go up the
stairs on the side of the building."

Red started to head for the door with Jacob at his
heels. As soon as they got outside Jacob asked, "Red, what is it?
What's wrong?"

Red turned to Jacob and said, "Esmeralda's... it's a cat-
house. I've got to get her out of there."

"I'm going with you," Jacob said. Red started to protest
but Jacob cut him off. "There's no arguing about it. We need to
watch out for each other, right?"

They dropped off their things upstairs and changed
into civilian clothes. Red reached into the bottom of his duffel
and pulled out a pistol, a Mauser C96 he had taken off of a dead
German officer after the Battle of Aisne. He looked hard at
Jacob and said, "I can't ask you to do this Jake. This could get
messy."

Jacob just nodded. "I know," he said. "All the more
reason I need to go.

Esmeralda's was situated in a large wooden house on
the south end of Ohio Street. There was a smell in the air
from the canal and a coat of ash on the street from the nearby
foundry. As they approached the front door they were eyed by
a stocky man wearing a wool overcoat and bowler. Jacob nodded

to the man who just grunted and stepped aside, but not before staring at Red, who had a snap brimmed hat pulled low over his eyes.

They entered a dimly lit anteroom. There was a heavy-set woman seated at a small table. It would have been hard to tell her age given the copious amount of makeup she had painted on her face. She was obviously wearing a wig too, which had seen better days. She looked up at Jacob and Red with mild suspicion.

"Can I help you gentlemen?" she asked in a husky voice. There was a trace of an accent, something vaguely European.

"Denny King sent us," Jacob replied. It had been agreed that he would do most of the talking, given Red's level of distress.

She stood up, adjusting a silk dress that was too tight on her, without taking her eyes off of them. She seemed to consider them and then gave a small nod. "So, you know where you are then?"

"Yes ma'am," Jacob said. "My friend and I are just back from the war and Denny King said this was the best place to go for a home coming."

She seemed neither pleased nor grateful for the compliment to her establishment. "Monsieur King has a big mouth," she huffed out. "Come with me." She turned and led them through a beaded curtain into a larger, although equally poorly lit, parlor. "Wait here," she said. And then she waddled up a narrow staircase.

When she returned she was trailed by four girls. Two of them were too old to be Red's sisters. The third girl had an olive complexion, too dark to be named Maureen or Molly Doyle. The fourth girl may have been young enough, but there was a hardness about her eyes that told Jacob she had been at this for a while or had otherwise led a difficult life. To be sure he looked at Red, who just shook his head and grimaced.

The madam let out a sigh. "What's the problem?" she asked.

"Well..." Jacob began. He could feel the perspiration under his shirt. "It's just that we were looking for..." his voice trailed off.

The madam said something under her breath and then, "A thousand pardons," she said mockingly. "Are your Lordships less than pleased?"

Red started to speak up but Jacob put a hand on his arm. He could feel his friend getting tenser by the moment. He knew he had to speed things up. His eyes swept the four girls and he said. "No offense to these fine ladies." He pulled out a roll of bills and flashed it at the madam. He and Red had pooled their money, Jacob suggesting they might have to make a show of it. "Do you have anyone . . . a little younger?" In the following silence he could here Red gritting his teeth.

The madam frowned and gave Red a look. She turned to one of the older women and said, "Get the other two."

When the woman came back she was trailed by two girls. Something was wrong, Jacob knew. He knew one was

Maureen right away by her resemblance to Red. The other girl was obviously too old to be Molly.

Before they had even reached the foot of the stairs Red had pulled off his hat. "Maureen!" he yelled.

A mix of emotions crossed Maureen's face, confusion, recognition, joy and then fear all within a matter of seconds. "Tim?" she finally asked.

"Maureen, get you things. We're leaving."

"How touching." The madam interrupted the reunion. "The young lady owes me money for room and board. And since her sister ran off last week she owes me for her too."

Red turned to the madam, his face flushed and his scars white. "Hag!" he yelled. "What kind of evil game are you running here?"

"No game," she replied. "Two young girls show up at my doorstep looking for work. I take them in out of the kindness of my heart and they steal from me and eat me out of house and home."

Maureen was shaking her head but couldn't speak. Tears were rolling down her cheeks, smearing her makeup.

The madam went on. "I hired them to clean and look after the girls but they couldn't even do that! Then the little one runs off and this one," she gestured towards Maureen. "This is the only way she can make it up."

Red was apoplectic now. "You rotten old whore..." he started. No one had seen the man from the porch come into the room behind Red. Out of the corner of his eye Jacob saw the club come down and strike Red on the back of his head. Red went down in a heap and Maureen screamed. The man gave Red a kick in the side and then turned towards Jacob. He raised the club and started to rush him, not seeing that Jacob had removed his old bayonet from his boot. He had hesitated on that cold morning in France and almost paid for it with his life. The ape barely seemed to register the glint of metal as Jacob plunged it up into his heart, just like he had been trained to do. His momentum carried him into Jacob and the two men crashed into a side table and then toppled onto the floor. Jacob pushed the man off of him and stood up. The man was clutching his chest, vainly trying to stem the flow of blood.

The girls were in shock. They stood with open mouths or hands over their eyes. Finally the madam moved, she backed over to another table and reached for a telephone.

"Stop!" Red yelled, rising to his feet. The madam looked from her thug to Red and then saw that he had drawn his pistol.

She cursed and said, "What have you done? You can't . . . you won't get away with this! Half of the local police precinct are customers here!" She picked up the phone.

The gun went off, once, twice. The madam rolled over the table and then she too fell to the floor. One of the younger girls screamed. Jacob looked at Red, he was wild eyed and looked like he might shoot someone else. He walked over to his friend and gently put his hand on Red's arm and lowered the weapon. He looked at Maureen and said, "Maureen, get your things. We have to go, now."

Maureen wiped her eyes and ran up the stairs. The two men stood with the five prostitutes and their two dying employers. The younger girl, the one who had come in with Maureen, was sobbing and shaking. One of the older women finally spoke up, "You son of a bitch. What are we supposed to do now?"

Red seemed to have come out of his funk. He looked at the girl who had spoken in disbelief.
"What?' he said.

"I said; what are we supposed to do now?" She looked more angry than upset.

Maureen was rushing down the stairs with a small suit-case. Red took a final, contemptuous look around the room and said, "Go be a whore somewhere else!" Then he turned and left with his sister and his best friend.

CHAPTER 4

Buffalo New York, 1919 - 1928

At first, Jacob didn't leave Buffalo because he wanted to help Red and Maureen find Molly. The first week after the incident at Esmeralda's the two men scoured the city, hospitals, orphanages, convents and other places but came up empty. The whole time they checked the local newspapers for mention of an investigation into the incident at Esmeralda's. After a front page article the day after it happened the press and the police seemed to lose interest. The First Ward could be a violent place and given the nature and reputation of the brothel it was soon just a memory. With their separation pay from the service almost gone and the room above Mahar's Tavern not suited to a long term stay, Red sought out Denny King looking for work. They found him downstairs at the bar, as usual, and he told Red he could start as a grain scooper right away.

After he told Red where to report the next morning, King turned to Jacob and said, "What about you, young fella? We could always use a strapping lad like yourself."

Red was about to answer for him but Jacob cut him off.

"Sure, I could use the work," he said.

Red raised his eyebrows and considered Jacob with a smile. Jacob knew that the search for Molly had hit a stone wall but there was something else; he realized he was falling in love with Maureen. She was still somber and reserved, grieving for the loss of her father and the disappearance of her sister. but once she had been removed from the service of Madame Esmeralda, Jacob saw a beautiful, innocent girl with a disarming (if infrequent) smile and the bluest eyes he had ever seen. They sat up and talked at night after Red had fallen asleep, worn out from a long day of looking for Molly, and part of Jacob knew he had to stay.

Working in the holds of the grain ships and in the elevators was suffocating, back breaking work. The men had been told that under no conditions were they to smoke or strike a match for any reason, a lone spark might send the whole place up in flames and them with it. Red's respiratory problems didn't help either. He was often short of breath and struggled to make it through the work day. It was work though and soon they saved enough to rent a small apartment in a building on South Park. The plan was for Jacob to get a place of his own as soon as he had saved enough money. Red insisted that he stay with them as long as he wanted; he owed him at least that much.

A week later came Maureen's revelation. Jacob and Red had returned from work one evening to find her in tears and when Red pressed her she retreated to the bedroom and closed the door. It was only after a few hours that Red was able to quietly enter the room and speak to his sister. Maureen was with child. Jacob had never heard Red and Maureen discuss what exactly had happened during her time at the brothel, part of him didn't want to know, but instead of being repulsed by her plight it only made him more sympathetic

A few nights later, as Jacob and Red were making their way back to the flat after work, Jacob worked up the courage to propose a solution. "I need to ask you something--" he started hesitantly.

"What's on your mind lad?" Red responded.

"I guess I ..." Jacob hesitated again, searching for words.

"What is it Jake?" Red said turning to his friend. Red, obviously, had a lot on his mind recently and had been in a sour mood.

Jacob found his resolve and decided the direct approach would be best. "I'd like to ask you for your blessing."

Red stopped in his tracks and looked directly at Jacob. "My what?"

"I'd like to marry Maureen."

Red frowned and then removed his cap. Slowly a smile played across his face. "Are ye daft?"

"Listen Red, this isn't something I..."

Red interrupted him. "Who is this I'm speaking to? Saint Jacob, patron of soldiers and fallen women?"

"Red, just..."

"You owe us nothing!" Red exclaimed. "You saved my life and got her out of that shit hole."

"This isn't about obligation or debts or charity!" Jacob raised his voice over Red's. When he was convinced he had Red's attention he added, "I'm in love with your sister you jackass."

The two men stared at each other for a moment and then Red put his cap back on. "By God you are daft," he said. "But if I can live with it I guess Maureen can as well." He turned towards home and added, "I suppose we should get her opinion on the matter."

Maureen's reaction was not unlike her brother's. She had been more than shocked and terrified by her situation, and her first instinct was to assume that Jacob was motivated by pity. At first, she refused to hear it and then broke down and cried. Red excused himself to go down to the bar and then Jacob spent the next few hours convincing Maureen that he was motivated by love. She seemed skeptical at first but he persisted and at the end she smiled through the tears and fell into his embrace.

Jacob took a week's pay and went to a jewelry store on Main Street. He didn't have enough for a ring so he settled for a heart shaped pendant for Maureen. With Red and a few friends as witnesses they were married at the courthouse on Niagara Square.

Jacob had sent a letter home relating selective parts of his story. He explained that he had met a nice girl, landed a good job and wouldn't be returning to the farm. He begged for his parents' understanding. A month later he received a response, a tersely worded message from his mother, Iris. She said she hoped he would change his mind, as he was needed at the farm and one day he would inherit the land. The thought of returning to the farm suddenly left Jacob cold. His parents could be difficult and the prospect of being responsible for the farm and his simple brother Willie after they were gone was daunting. His sister, Constance, had already left the nest while he was in France. She and her husband John had moved to Jamestown where John went to work at his uncle's lumber mill.

Seven months later Adam was born.

^^^

After a few years of paying their dues as scoopers and much badgering of Denny King, they found other work at the elevators. Red got a job loading trucks and Jacob became a machinist. Red still had his good days and his bad days, but now he could at least make it through a whole day without almost suffocating.

Adam's earliest memories of Life on Chicago Street were happy ones. He spent the day with his mother, who would keep house and take in laundry from some of the neighbors to help out. In the evenings his father and Uncle Red would come home from work tired and dirty from a long day. But after they cleaned up and ate dinner there were always stories and wrestling until it was time for bed.

When he was old enough to start school, his mother would walk him the five blocks to the nearest public school.

She wanted him to attend St. Aloysious as her brother had, but Adam had never been baptized, because his mother had married a Protestant. His second year Adam told her he wasn't a baby anymore and he could walk to school with his friends from the neighborhood. Maureen reluctantly agreed, although for the first few weeks of the school year she followed Adam, Johnny Keil, and Joe O'Rourke from a distance.

A few more years went by and there was talk of buying a bigger house, farther away from the canal and the bustle and smell of the old First Ward. Then in the fall of '28 things changed drastically. The Scoopers union was consolidated with the dock workers union and the new leadership made immediate, drastic changes. One of the more noticeable was the disappearance of Denny King. He had told them the transition would be a smooth one and he would always look out for their interests. This placated his charges for a while, Denny was a blowhard and a bit of a drunk, but you always knew where he stood. Then one day there was a notice at the hall that Denny was no longer the hiring man for the local and all assignments and inquiries were to go through the dock workers' secretary. Denny had simply vanished and that added to the feeling of unease among the men.

It didn't help that the secretary of the dock workers local was a hard, sullen man whom none of the men had ever seen put in a day's work on the docks or in the elevators. He was also usually surrounded by his "associates," a rough looking bunch of thick-necked thugs whose jobs seemed mostly to be glaring at and intimidating anyone who approached the secretary. Jobs were reassigned and it didn't take long to realize that the new system of hiring was based on favoritism, connections and kickbacks to the stewards and the secretary. Grumbling was discouraged and more than one man found himself being threatened or roughed up for speaking out. Red found out he would have to go back into the ship's holds as a scooper. He and Jacob and the others were reaching the limit of what they could stand. Winter was just a few months away. In order to ensure that there would be grain to process all year, the "Winter Fleet" would line up at the docks before Lake Erie froze over. That meant there was work year round which was good, but add the cold and the damp to the already stifling conditions and it could be a miserable experience, especially for someone in Red's condition.

One day on their way out of the elevator in mid-October, a man approached them with a flyer. Jacob thought he recognized the man from the docks or the elevator. He was tall and thin and had always seemed quiet and thoughtful.

"Meeting tonight at the Scooper's Hall," he said, handing the flyer to Red.

"What is it?" Jacob asked.

Red scanned the flyer and frowned. Then his face took on a more thoughtful look. "It's about worker's rights," he finally said. He handed Jacob the flyer. Jacob looked it over. At the top a the page, in bold print was a question; *Who is looking out for you?*

Jacob looked at the man, who was off down the street still handing out flyers. He folded it up and put it in his pocket. "We should talk about this," he said.

After an unusually quiet dinner, Maureen sensed that something was going on so she sent Adam upstairs to do his lessons. Jacob took out the flyer and put it on the table.

"Rabble rousers," Red said without conviction.

"They do make a few good points," Jacob said.

Maureen shook her head. "I don't like it. Hasn't there been enough trouble?"

Jacob sighed and took the flyer in his hand. "It's just that..." his voice trailed off.

"How much more are we supposed to take?" Red picked up. His change of tune seemed to catch the other two by surprise and they just looked at him. "The more I think about it, the more sense it makes."

"Tim..." Maureen started.

"No Sis, I mean, do you think the owner of the elevator gives a damn about what goes on as long as the work gets done? And these people at the Dock Workers Hall, they're nothing but a bunch of criminals if you ask me."

"What's the harm of hearing what they have to say?" Jacob added.

^^^

Late that night Adam was awoken by the sound of the front door opening downstairs and then being slammed shut.

Next, he could hear his parents' voices; they were trying to speak in hushed tones but he could hear the distress in their voices. He crept to the landing and looked down into the parlor. His mother was holding a cloth to his father's head. Blood had trickled from Jacob's hairline down the side of his face. His hat was missing and his coat was torn.

"I don't know. They came in swinging clubs and pipes. Me and a few of the other guys made it out the back door. I thought Red was behind me but when I got to the alley he wasn't there."

Adam looked at his mother. She was fighting back the tears but was focused on Jacob. "Who was it?" she asked.

"They were wearing scarves and masks," Jacob said wincing. "I recognized one of 'em though. It was the gang from the Dock Worker's Hall."

There was already an electricity to the air and things seemed on edge. It came to a crescendo suddenly when the front window exploded in a shower of glass and a rock landed in the middle of the room. The rock had what looked like a red handprint on it. Maureen screamed and suddenly looked up and saw Adam at the top of the stairs. A look of terror mixed with determination crossed her face as she ran up and lifted him off the ground and into the back room. Adam could still hear the voices of the men outside from their hiding place.

"Avery! There's no work for Communists in this town!" The voice sounded hoarse, almost animalistic. "You'd best take your whore wife and clear out!"

Maureen couldn't help herself anymore. She pulled Adam tighter to her and broke down crying.

Jacob spent the rest of the night sitting by the barricaded door with one of Maureen's kitchen knives in his hand. At daybreak he told Maureen that he was going to look for Red but as he was pulling on his torn coat there was a knock on the door. It was the police. Red's body had been pulled from the canal a few hours ago.

The next day Red was laid to rest in a potter's field at the edge of the city. Jacob and Maureen packed Adam and what they could reasonably carry and took the last train to Cattaraugus County.

CHAPTER 5

B efore they left Buffalo that day Adam had only been outside of the city a handful of times, a few family picnics at the beach and an excursion to Niagara Falls. The train ride South was a new experience altogether, mile after mile of farms and small towns with what seemed like nothing but open spaces and woodland in between.

A cool breeze was blowing as they got off the train onto the platform at South Dayton. There were maybe eight to ten buildings in the whole town as far as Adam could see. No sooner had they secured their belongings from the porter than they were approached by a short stocky man in dirty bib overalls.

"Jacob!" the man exclaimed as a smile crossed his weather-creased face.

Jacob turned and recognized the man immediately. "Hal!" he said extending his right hand. "It's good to see you."

Hal shook Jacob's hand enthusiastically. "Damn son," he said, still grinning. "Look at you, all grown up." It was then that he looked past Jacob and saw Maureen. He blushed and removed his cap. "Pardon the language, ma'am. It's just that I haven't seen this young man in almost ten years."

Maureen smiled and said, "It's quite alright."

"Hal, this is my wife Maureen and my son Adam," Jacob said.

Hal bowed awkwardly to Maureen and then looked at Adam and smiled. "Hello there young man."

Adam stepped forward and offered his hand. He had never felt anything as rough and calloused as Hal's firm handshake. "Pleased to meet you," he said.

Jacob glanced around and then looked back at Hal. "Is it just you?" he asked.

Hal looked back at Jacob a little sheepishly and replied, "Well, your dad was having some work done on the cooling tank and couldn't leave..."

Hal went on to explain how Leon had been trying to modernize the dairy operation. He had purchased a milking machine and cooling tank, effectively increasing the production as well as reducing spoilage.

"Well I imagine you're anxious to be getting home," Hal said, taking one of the heavier suitcases.

Jacob hesitated for a moment, and then replied, "Yeah... you bet."

The '28 Ford Model AA truck was parked in front of the Depot. On the side door of the black truck it said 'Avery Farms' in block white lettering. The sides of the bed had been built up to a height of two feet, a special order from Jacob's father to the dealer, to handle the milk cans and other equipment.

Hal put the bags in the back of the truck and held out the key to Jacob. "There's only room for two in the cab. Why don't you and the missus ride up front and I'll hop in back with the lad?" He caught Adam's eye and winked.

"Nonsense," Jacob replied, waving off the keys. "You know the way a lot better than I do, and besides, I have to keep an eye on this one." He spun and grabbed Adam by the waist, hoisted him into the back of the truck then climbed in after him.

The ride to the farm took almost two hours. At first the way was smooth, well maintained two lane blacktop. Then it became increasingly slow and bumpy as Hal cut across some of the lesser traveled roads of Cattaraugus County. After at first enjoying the fresh October air, Adam felt a chill and then his stomach lurched with every bump the truck hit. Finally, when Adam was about ready to be sick, his father nudged his leg and said, "We're here."

Adam looked to his left. A wooden sign stood by the roadside.

The Hollow
Avery Farms

The lettering on the sign looked like it had been professionally done. As Adam looked closer he noticed that some of the letters and the white painted background were starting to flake.

The truck made its way slowly up the long tree lined drive. At the end it lurched to a halt and Hal shut the engine down. "Let's go," Jacob said. They climbed off the back of the truck and almost bumped into Hal, who had come around to get the bags. The sun had sunk below the western tree line, giving the air an additional chill. Suddenly, a breeze picked up and Adam could smell the scent of manure coming from the barn off in the distance. Some of the merchants in the first ward still used horse drawn wagons, so the smell was nothing new to Adam, but at the same time it was almost overpowering Jacob was helping Maureen out of the passenger side when a tall older man approached them.

Leon Avery stood six foot two inches tall and was thin as a rail. But despite his lack of bulk he moved with a sense of strength that had come from a lifetime of manual labor. Adam could see the resemblance between his father and his grandfather; the chief difference between the two men, besides their age, was the tell-tale red nose and rheumy eyes of a heavy drinker. Despite his young age, Adam had seen enough men in the ward who had succumbed to the call of John Barleycorn.

"Hello Father," Jacob said, offering his hand.

"Jacob, it's good to have you home," his father said taking his hand.

Out of the corner of his eye, Adam saw movement on the front porch of the house. He looked in that direction and saw a slight older woman. She had gray hair, pulled back in a bun and had gray, piercing eyes. Adam's first impression of his

grandmother, Iris, was that her outward expression was total-
ly devoid of warmth or joy. She stood on the porch and just
looked at the reunion with the same expression she would have
if she were about to begin some tiresome chore.

"Hello Ma," Adam heard Jacob say. Adam looked to his
father and then back at Iris. She hadn't moved or changed her
expression.

Adam felt Jacob's hand on his shoulder and his father
continued, "This is Maureen and Adam, my family."

Adam felt his grandfather's hand tousle his hair. He
looked up at the older man who towered above him. Leon
smiled and said, "Looks a little small and underfed. We'll take
care of that."
The gesture felt forced to Adam for some reason, as if the old
man were acting out of character.

"Father Avery." Maureen smiled and curtsied. Then she
turned and walked in the direction of the porch. "And Mother
Avery! It's so good to finally meet you."

Iris barely turned her head in Maureen's direction.
"You must be tired," she said quickly. "Hal! Take their bags to
Constance's old room."

Just then Adam saw a small, wiry man come around the
far corner of the house. He stood about five foot six and was
wearing dirty overalls. He had small deep set eyes and greasy
brown hair.

"Hello Jake," the small man said.

"Willy!" Jake said when he turned that way. "Come over

here and meet your sister-in-law and your nephew."

Jacob had told Adam about his brother Willy. He said that he was 'a little slow,' but that there wasn't a harder worker or better hunter in the county.

Willy took a step and then stopped and looked down in the direction of Maureen's feet.

"Pleased to meet you," he said quietly.

"Willie!" Iris' voice cut in. "Take the boy's suitcase up to your room."

"I thought he might spend the first few nights with us," Maureen said, drawing everyone's attention. Her words hung in the air. There was a silence that followed as Iris finally looked directly at her daughter-in-law.

"The boy's too old to be spending the night in his parents' room."

Again a silence. Adam sensed that Iris was not used to being contradicted.

"It's okay, Ma," Jacob said with a smile. "Let's give him a couple of nights to get acclimated."

Iris turned towards Jacob like she was going to say something and bit it off. Jacob had also told Adam about Iris and Leon. He explained that even though Iris had never gone into great detail about her childhood, she had explained that her family was very religious and very strict. She saw the world through a prism of hard work, family and sacrifice. Leon, on the other hand, had been raised on the very land where they were now standing. His own father had died when Leon was only twenty, leaving Leon to run the farm and take care of his mother and two younger sisters. Leon worked hard and had learned from that early age that nothing would be handed to him. He had worked for years to make the farm a success.

"Son," Jacob said. "Give me and Hal a hand with the bags."

Adam felt himself blushing against his will. He *was* too old to sleep in his parents' room. But he also knew that there was something about Willy that made him uneasy. "Yes sir," he said. He put his cap back on and picked up his bag and lowered his head.

Iris turned towards the door. "Well, you're late for supper," she said over her shoulder. "But I think I can fix you something to eat."

"Please let me help you Mother Avery." Maureen said climbing the stairs.

Iris opened the screen door and turned to Maureen. "That won't be necessary dear," she smiled without warmth. "I like to keep my kitchen to myself."

CHAPTER 6

If this was the life of a farmer, Adam thought the next day, you could keep it. His father had woken him up before sunrise in a chill, unfamiliar room and after a breakfast of lumpy oatmeal, it was off to help pick the last of the season's corn. Adam was too young to wield the long knife used to cut down the stalks, so his job was to collect and bundle the stalks where they would sit in the field and dry for a few days. Adam tried to stay close to his father but found himself falling farther behind the men cutting the corn as he struggled to collect the wet heavy stalks. He thought his uncle Willie was giving him disapproving looks so he quickened his pace. His father and four other field hands, including Hal were wordlessly toiling away with the knives, sweating despite the cool October air.

At midday his mother brought out a basket with cheese sandwiches and apples. The work party had gathered at the edge of the field for lunch, sitting under a large elm tree that had shed most of its leaves. Adam had never been so hungry in his life. His hands were sore and his back ached, but he said nothing. Instead he sat down on the ground next to his father and listened to his grandfather, who had arrived late, explain his plans for the near future.

"Some of the other farmers around Randolph have started a co-op," Leon said. "They built a refrigerated collection building right next to the train depot. We can ship fresh milk anywhere in the state overnight."

"Who's going to buy all the milk?" Jacob asked.

"City folk and people in the larger towns." Leon pulled a flask from his pocket, unscrewed the cap and took a sip. "The world's changed since you been away, son. We need to keep up. Just producing enough for ourselves and the locals isn't going to pay the mortgage."

Jacob looked quizzically at Leon. "Mortgage?" he asked. "I thought we owned the farm."

Leon squinted at something out in in the distance. "Had to borrow some to upgrade the farm," he said quietly. "The price of corn dropped the last few years and if we don't modernize..." his voice trailed off. Adam looked at his father, who said nothing but looked at his own father with concern.

"Get the hell away from me, you God damned half-wit!" a man's voice cried out.

Everyone turned to see what the commotion was. Emmett, one of the farm hands was face to face with Willie. Willie's right hand was on the handle of the large buck knife he wore in a sheath on his hip. Emmett was a head taller than Willie and looked like he was ready to fight.

"Calm down Emmett," Hal said, stepping towards the

two men. "What's this all about?"

"This half-wit says I'm not doing my share," Emmett said turning part way towards Hal. He turned back to Willie and added, "You better get your hand off that knife boy."

Willie just stared at Emmett, his face red. No one moved for a moment then Willie said, "Call me that again."

Emmett smirked and said, "Call you what? A half..."

The knife was out of the sheath in a flash. Emmett lost some of his bravado and took a step back with his hands up in front of him.

"Willie!" Leon barked. "Stop!"

Willie stopped in his tracks, still holding the knife out.

"Put that away!" Leon added. He stepped between the two men glaring at Willie until he sheathed the knife. He then wheeled around and faced Emmett.

"Mr. Avery..." Emmett started.

"You're fired!" Leon spat.

Emmett shook his head in disbelief. He tried to make eye contact with Leon but couldn't. "Sir... I'm sorry..." he stammered.

"Not as sorry as you're going to be if you're not off my land before night fall." Leon added. His face was flushed now.

Emmett swallowed and looked away. He picked up his hat and started walking back towards the barn. The silence was palpable. No one seemed able to look at anyone else. Finally Hal sidled up to Leon. "Sir, beggin' your pardon, but Emmett's been with us..." The words stopped when Leon turned and glared at him. Leon then looked at Willie, who had a smirk on his face. Leon walked right up to Willie and slapped him hard across the face. Willie hit the ground with a whimper. Adam thought he looked like a beaten dog, lying at Leon's feet.

"Pull that knife again," Leon said walking away, "you'll get worse than that."

The crew went back to work but now all conversation had ceased, the confrontation had cast a pall on an already hard day. Adam had lost track of time, only a few breaks were taken to get a drink of water and stretch his aching back. He kept waiting for someone to call time, but no one did and eventually the sun fell behind the tree line, yet the men worked on. Adam's thoughts had turned dark. He actually contemplated leaving the field and going back to the house, yet he didn't want to disappoint his father or raise the ire of his grandfather or Uncle Willie. Just when he thought he couldn't lift another bunch of stalks, and the sun had almost completely set, he felt his father's hand on his shoulder.

"That's a good days work son," Jacob said. "Let's go get some supper."

Despite his raw hands and aching body Adam smiled up at his father and nodded.

Leon, Jacob, Willie and Adam took turns washing up at the pump out in front of the house. As Adam washed his hands in the chill October air he realized his stomach was growling and he couldn't wait for dinner. Hal and the three remaining field hands had retired to the bunk house next to the barn where they would take their supper and retire for the evening.

The first thing Adam noticed as they took their seats at the kitchen table was that his mother looked angry and his grandmother had an icy air about her. The men were already in a somber mood, given the incident at lunch time so the meal was eaten in almost complete silence. As dinner concluded Adam could feel his eyes getting heavy. His father's voice brought him back around.

"Adam, why don't you help your mother and grand-mother clear the dishes?" Jacob said.

"Nonsense," Leon piped in, whiskey glass raised halfway to his mouth, "that's woman's work."

Adam looked to his father for direction. Jacob just shrugged and looked sheepishly at Maureen who just looked down at her half eaten dinner.

Adam went upstairs and got undressed and collapsed onto the cot that had been set up next to his parents' bed in the small front bedroom. He fell asleep almost immediately. A short time later though he awoke to hear his parents speaking in hushed tones.

"He should be in school," he heard Maureen say. "What kind of life will he have without an education?"

Adam didn't enjoy school. But he knew that in the modern world those who could read and write were better off than those who couldn't. He had seen classmates pulled out of school to help support their families. They mostly worked long hours at menial, dangerous jobs, with only a bleak future ahead of them, toiling away in sweatshops or out on the streets. Even though he didn't miss the drudgery of schoolwork, he didn't like the thought of falling behind.

"I know," Jacob said softly. "But they got a late start this year and they could use the help. We can enroll him at the start of the year."

"That's not what your mother said!" Maureen hissed through her teeth. "She said he can learn all he needs about life right here on the farm."

"Shh," Jacob said. "It'll be alright. I'll talk to her tomorrow."

And with that Adam's parents fell silent. He was worried about the obvious tension between his mother and grandmother, but the day's work was still weighing on him and he soon drifted off again.

A short time later though, Adam had no idea what time it was, he was awakened by a pain in his intestines. The stew Iris had prepared for dinner had been bland but filling and he had wolfed down two helpings. He realized he had to go to the privy. As he silently rose out of the cot he heard a sound outside the window. He stepped over to it and looked down in the front yard. The moon was shining brightly that night and in the bluish light he could make out his uncle Willie washing his hands at the pump. Adam didn't want to run into Willie but he had to go badly. He decided he would creep down the stairs and go out the back kitchen door.

The sound of the pump working had stopped so he

double timed it down the stairs and turned to go into the kitchen. He was halfway to the door to the back yard when it swung open and there stood Willie. His hands were dripping wet and he was holding something in his right that looked like the jawbone of an animal. His eyes were deep set and his coat was covered with blood.

"What are you doin' boy?" Willie said.

Adam was struck speechless. Willie made a half-hearted effort to conceal the bone and then said, "Are you deaf? What are you doin'?"

Adam swallowed and said, "I need to use the privy." His voice sounded weak to himself.

"This time of night?" Wille said, taking a step forward. Even though Willie was in his late twenties, he was barely six inches taller that Adam. That didn't reduce the level of menace though especially when Willie opened his coat and revealed the ever present knife on his hip.

Adam tried to be brave. He stood his ground and tried to look his uncle in the eye. When that failed he tried something different. He clutched at his abdomen and bent over. He pushed down as hard as he could and broke wind.

Willie frowned and stepped aside. "Damn it son, hurry up." But as Adam tried to pass, Willie grabbed his arm and turned Adam to face him. "Just don't go tellin' anybody what you seen tonight." His face was inches from Adam's and his breath was hot and stale.

"No sir, I won't." He replied quietly. He broke away

and went out the back door.

CHAPTER 7

Adam was still exhausted in the morning when he
woke up. He wanted to tell his father what he had
seen the previous night, but he was truly terrified of Willie and
decided to wait for a while, if ever he mustered the courage to
bring it up. Breakfast was better this morning, hotcakes with
maple syrup. Adam's stomach had almost fully recovered from
last night's distress but his nerves were on edge so his appetite
was lacking. To Maureen's credit, she was putting on a good
show, trying to act cheerful as if yesterday's disagreement with
Iris had never happened.

After breakfast he followed Jacob out to the barn where
Leon and Hal were trying to get the tractor started. Hal was
doing something to the engine while Leon was in the driver's
seat red-faced and cursing. Willie was nowhere in sight. Today,
Jacob had told Adam, they would go out into the field with
husking pegs. He showed him what looked like a short blade on
a wooden handle with a wrist strap that they would use to bring
the corn into the crib where it would dry.

Adam noticed that his grandfather had stopped what he

was doing and was climbing down off the tractor. Something had caught his attention. Adam turned in the direction Leon was looking and saw a man walking up the drive. It was hard to tell the man's age. He was tall and thin and looked hungry and tired. As he approached Leon he took off his hat. His thinning hair was plastered down to his scalp.

"Good morning Earl," Leon said with an unnatural pleasant tone to his voice.

"Mr. Avery?" The man nodded in return. He looked at Adam and then Jacob. "Jacob," he said, "nice to see you back home."

Adam glanced up at his father who looked like he was struggling to recognize the man. After a moment he smiled and said, "Thanks Mr. Johnston. Good to see you too."

"What can we do for you Earl?" Leon interrupted. "We've got a full day's work ahead of us and we really need to get started."

"Yes... sorry, sir," Earl Johnston started. "This is kind of important. I was hoping we could have a quick word..."

Leon looked down at the man impatiently. He seemed to drop some of his earlier affability. "Well... what's so important then?"

Johnston glanced around. He looked at Adam and Jacob like he wanted to speak to Leon in private.

"Earl," Leon said impatiently, "you can say anything in front of my family that you want to say to me."

Johnston's hands tightened on the brim of his hat. He

finally looked up at Leon. "Well . . . I've decided to accept your offer, Mr. Avery."

Leon smirked slightly, "And what offer was that?"

A look of disbelief came over Johnston's features. "Surely you remember," he shot a glance at Jacob and then looked back at Leon, "your offer for my land."

"Ah yes." Leon nodded. "That was a while ago Earl."

"Six months ago, yes sir." Johnston replied.

"Why now? What changed your mind?"

Johnston looked at the ground and shook his head. "Last night... a coyote got into the chicken coop... killed all of 'em."

"Tsk, tsk, tsk," Leon noised shaking his head. "What about your crops? Can't you sell enough to make it through the winter?"

"That's just it Mr. Avery," Johnston looked like he was near tears. "It was a lean yield. I don't know why but the corn and potatoes never grew like they should have."

Adam was looking at his father. He thought of Willie and their run in last night. He was sure Willie had killed those chickens. He had a darker thought then; had Willie somehow tampered with Johnston's crops? Just then he noticed Willie had joined the circle and was looking directly at him. Adam's blood froze.

"Well, that is some hard luck Earl," Leon said.

Adam looked at Johnston. He could tell he was trying to maintain his dignity despite it all. He shot a glance at Willie who seemed to sense it and looked back at him immediately. Adam felt sick to his stomach.

"I'm afraid I'm a little short though Earl, "Leon continued. "I've had to update some equipment and I just can't get my hands on that kind of money right now. So if you'll excuse us." Leon turned to walk away.

"I'd take installments!" Johnston blurted out.

Leon turned back to the man and half smiled. He looked at him as if he were considering something. "I don't know Earl. It's going to be a long winter for us too."

Johnston looked panic stricken. "I'll take a lower offer," he said pleadingly.

Leon considered for a moment. "Fine, I'll give you a thousand dollars."

Johnston looked dumbfounded. "Mr. Avery... that's less than half of..."

"Earl," Leon interrupted him sharply, "that's a thousand more than you'll get from the bank when they foreclose and put you and your family out."   Several emotions seemed to cross Johnston's face in quick sequence. He went from disbelief to embarrassment to anger and then finally resignation.

And that was how the Avery's acquired the parcel of land next to theirs. The joy Adam would feel escaping his grandparents' house and the close proximity to Willie would always be tempered by the way the land came to be available.

CHAPTER 8

Compared to his grandparent's house the Johnston's house was nothing more than a three room cabin. The walls and floors were bare wood and the windows were cheaply constructed and drafty. Even though Adam felt for the Johnston's and the hand his uncle Willie may have had in their predicament, he found the chance to live away from his extended family elating.

Maureen's mood seemed to improve slightly. She remained drawn within herself but set about the house cleaning it top to bottom and putting out the few possessions she had brought from Buffalo in an attempt to make the house their own. Jacob worked on the outside of the house, fixing a leak in the roof and tuckpointing the chimney. The windows, he said, he would be able to insulate with materials from his father's property.

The fields at the former Johnston farm were deemed a lost cause by Leon, and would be seen to in the spring. There was still plenty of work to do at the Avery farm however, mostly finishing the late harvest and getting the place ready for winter. For Adam, that meant daily sunrise treks to his grand-parents' house for breakfast and then a full day of work. At Maureen's instance though, and with Iris' silent disapproval, Adam and Jacob returned to their own home for dinner. Maureen proved to be quite adept at converting the humble supplies her in-laws sent over into a hearty, satisfying meal.

Adam's Mother was still pushing the idea of school on his father. Jacob had attended school in Little Valley, fifteen miles away, through the eighth grade. Then, he explained to Maureen, he was thirteen years old and expected to assume the duties of a full time farmer. One day, Leon had explained to him, he would be the head of the household and inherit the farm. But the older Jacob got, the more the idea of spending his entire life in The Hollow left him discouraged. It wasn't until he ran off and joined the army that Jacob told his parents how he felt. It wasn't something the Averys did. Leon had been born and raised on the same land and Iris' whole life seemed to be one of tireless work. For the most part, his sister Connie towed the family line. Occasionally she would break out and actually seem to enjoy things. She met her husband John at a barn dance after Jacob had shipped out and shortly after they were married moved to Jamestown where John's uncle owned a sawmill. Willie, well he was just simple. Adam wondered if the thought of having to look after Willie for the rest of his life had anything to do with Jacob's decision to flee the farm.

While they were clearing the dinner dishes one night, Maureen asked once again about enrolling Adam at school. Jacob said he would speak to his parents again regarding Adam's schooling. Maureen, uncharacteristically, bristled at her husband. "What's there to speak about?" she said, staring at Jacob. "He's our son. I won't have him growing up uneducated."

"I know darlin', It's just that my parents..." Jacob struggled to find the words to explain himself. "It's different out here. You're expected to grow up faster."

Maureen crossed her arms in front of herself. "Well then, how old do you think Adam will be when he runs off?"

Jacob blinked and looked back at Maureen. He looked frustrated and ready to lash out at his wife. Then, just as quickly, he took a deep breath and spoke calmly; "I know you're upset. I know none of this has been easy. We just have to make the best of the situation."

Maureen grimaced and looked away. Jacob continued; "We have a roof over our heads and food in the larder. You and Adam are safe and you have no Idea what that means to me."

A single tear rolled down Maureen's cheek. She unfolded her arms and then walked across the room and threw them around Jacob's neck. Adam who had been listening quietly from the table, breathed a sigh of relief.

One concession Maureen did make was Sunday dinner at her in-laws' house. Maureen and Iris seemed to be able to tolerate each other's company long enough to make the dinners palatable. Adam could still sense the tension and he would often imagine his uncle Willie was staring at him or worse, at Maureen. Grandpa Leon would usually start the evening in a good mood but could become sullen once he was in his cups. Jacob did his best to keep the conversation moving and the family engaged. He would make sure his family was excused and on their way before Leon became truly obnoxious. Adam took the dinners as a hopeful sign that things were getting better.

That sense of calm was shattered one Sunday shortly after Thanksgiving. Maureen had mentioned that Adam would need new clothes for school which prompted Iris to drop her fork loudly on her plate.

"We're having a hard enough time keeping food on the table and paying the hands. Yet you insist on forwarding this extravagance," Iris said.

The corners of Maureen's mouth tightened. "I hardly see your grandson's education as an extravagance," she said.

Iris shook her head and said, "I had hoped you would have come around and realized you don't live in the city anymore." She paused and looked from Maureen to Jacob. "Have you thought this through? It's a thirty mile round trip to Little Valley! How is he going to get there?"

Maureen sat up straighter and replied in a calm conciliatory tone, "Well I thought perhaps Jacob could teach me to drive and while I'm out I could pick up supplies and do any marketing that needed to be done."

Adam glanced at his father and saw what appeared to be a look of concern. Maureen surely must have run this idea past Jacob, but he seemed surprised she had brought it up at this moment.

Iris was having none of it however. "Nonsense!" she spat. "We can do those things without driving all the way to Little Valley. Besides, Father needs the truck to carry out his grand dairy scheme." She finished by pointing a long thin finger at her husband at the other end of the table.

Adam shot a look at Leon who just sat tight lipped, staring into his glass. Clearly the way Iris said what she said meant that she was not entirely behind his plan.

"Honestly child," Iris went on. "How could you be so selfish?"

Now Adam looked at his parents on the other side of the table. He's expected a reaction from his mother but Maureen just sat expressionless. Jacob on the other hand was staring daggers at Iris.

"Mother..." he started to say raising his hand. Maureen moved swiftly then, placing her hand on Jacob's forearm and stopping him from continuing. Jacob turned to her with a vexed expression. The room was eerily silent for a moment until Maureen spoke,

"I apologize, Mother Avery," she said, eyes downcast. "I'm afraid I hadn't thought it through."

Iris appeared to bite something off that she was going to say. Instead she nodded and continued eating. The rest of the meal was spent in relative silence and went gratefully quickly. As soon as they could Jacob, Maureen and Adam excused themselves and made the trek back to their own home.

"It's all right dear," Maureen said, breaking the silence

about half way along the way. "I'll get my hands on as many books as I can and teach the boy myself if I have to."

Adam was a few steps behind his parents and barely heard what his mother had said. Jacob said nothing in reply. He just put his arm around Maureen and pulled her close.

CHAPTER 9

Winter settled in over the Hollow, bitter cold and dreary. Maureen had managed to acquire a few used grammar and math text books from a school in Jamestown. They were old and worn but she was determined that Adam would get some kind of education. A few hours a day were set aside for his lessons. She had also scrounged up a copy of *The Adventures of Tom Sawyer.* The winter nights were long and Adam devoured the book in no time at all.

Most mornings Adam would accompany Jacob to his grandparents' farm, where they would help out in the dairy barn. Adam had avoided the dairy barn as long as he could. He didn't know how anyone could stand the stench of cow manure that hung over the barn. Now here he was ankle deep in it. There had been a livery stable near their home in Buffalo, some of the peddlers and merchants still used horse drawn wagons. On a hot summer day the smell from the livery could be over-powering, but then the wind would shift and the slightly less unpleasant odors from the foundry or the mills would replace it. Still the livery couldn't compare to the stench emanating from the thirty some odd cows standing in their own shit.

Adam's favorite times were spent with his father, working around their own home. Jacob had set about making the
house more livable and Adam was his eager assistant. Windows
were glazed and caulked, Cracks were sealed and warped wall
and floor boards were replaced. More and more the simple
house felt like a home.

The short winter days and long cold nights passed
by like a dream. Once Adam got used to working in the dairy
barn the tasks seemed easier and the days more bearable. After
work it was home to a hot meal and the company of his parents.
Sundays his mother would make him say the rosary. Jacob did
not partake, but he insisted Adam honor his mother's desire
for some kind of religious indoctrination and then he and his
father would go sledding or hunting with his uncle Willie.
Willie seemed much more tolerant of Adam now, perhaps he
trusted that his secrets were safe. Or maybe it was the fact that
Willie was in his element out in the woods. At first Adam was
only allowed to keep quiet and observe, but after a while and
with some needling of his father he was taught how to use a
.22 caliber rifle. Willie and Jacob used shotguns and were after
deer, but soon Adam had become proficient enough to bag a few
rabbits.

One Sunday at dinner the family was discussing the
newly passed Volstead act, prohibiting the production and sale
of alcohol. Leon grumbled that the government had no business telling a grown man how to conduct his life. "They talk

about wine all through the God damned Bible," he claimed. Adam noticed his mother wince at Leon's blasphemy. Iris just glared across the table at her husband. "I'll be damned if I let them nanny me!" Leon exclaimed. True to his word, he soon found a source of homemade hooch from a nearby source.

Finally March came and with it a lasting thaw. It was time to get the fields ready. Maureen was pressed into helping out in the dairy barn with Iris and Hal while Adam and his father would be working with Willie, Leon, and the three remaining farmhands breaking up the ground for the upcoming seeding.

The third day the party was just about to head out, and Leon was just starting the tractor when two cars rolled up the drive. As they drew closer Adam saw the lead car had the words *Cattaraugus County Sheriff* painted on the side. The second car was a newer model sedan.

The cars came to a halt in front of the barn and two men got out. The driver was older, somewhere in his fifties. He was a large man, tall and stout with a greying bushy mustache. The man exiting the passenger side bore a slight resemblance to the driver, only younger and not as heavy. They both wore badges on their brown jackets. A smallish man with wirerimmed glasses climbed out of the second car. He wore a shirt and tie under an old leather jacket and paused as he straightened his Stetson hat.

Leon had climbed down off the tractor and looked irritated. "Sheriff," he said as he looked at the older man with the badge.

"Hello Leon," the Sheriff said flatly. He managed a slight smile, the corners of his mouth barely turning up. He jerked a thumb over his shoulder at the man in the leather coat. "This here's Mr. Kraft from the Farm Bureau."

"I know who he is," Leon said, with a disapproving glance in the man's direction.

The Sheriff looked at Jacob. "Hello Jake. I heard you were back."

"Sheriff Ferguson," Jacob nodded.

Ferguson scratched his ear, "Didn't you play Legion ball against my boy here?" he gestured towards the deputy with him.

"I did." Jacob tuned towards the deputy, "Silas, isn't it?"

The deputy nodded and grinned. "Still got that mark on your leg from where I spiked you at second base?"

Jacob smiled and said, "Nah, that faded away a long time ago."

Adam looked at his father. He could tell he was holding something back.

"What brings you all the way out here Ed?" Leon interrupted.

Sheriff Edward Ferguson looked back at Leon. "Right," he said. He turned towards Kraft, the Farm Bureau man and crooked his finger. Kraft stepped forward, producing a sheaf of papers from his jacket pocket.

"Mr. Avery, I'm afraid there's a problem with the milk

you've been selling."

"Nonsense!" Leon snapped. "It's cooled and refrigerated from the get go."

Kraft stopped in his tracks. Despite the chill morning air, a bead of sweat rolled down his temple.

"That's not the issue, Mr. Avery," Kraft said.

Leon took a step towards Kraft. Sheriff Ferguson move to block his path. "Easy Leon," Ferguson growled.

Leon was apoplectic. His face was turning redder by the minute. "If the milk's gone bad it's at the other end! Why aren't you bothering the distributors?"

Kraft held up the papers. "It's your herd Mr. Avery." He had seemed to gain some resolve with the Sheriff between himself and Leon. "It's a Bovine virus. The milk is tainted at the source."

Leon frowned. "Let me see that," he reached towards Kraft. At first Ferguson went to block him but after shooting Leon a disapproving look he relented.

Leon took the sheaf of papers and started to read the top page. He flipped to the second page and started to shake his head. "This can't be right," he said. "Every head in the barn is as healthy as can be."

"They may appear healthy, Mr. Avery," Kraft said, "but the virus is highly contagious and from all the tests we've run it looks like your whole herd may be infected."

"What?" Leon sputtered. His face was fully flushed now. "What are you saying?"

Kraft grimaced and exhaled. "I'm afraid you'll have to destroy the herd," he said.

"No, no, no," Leon was shaking his head again. "I won't... you can't..." He threw the papers towards Kraft and took a step forward. Ferguson stepped directly in front of Leon and put a large hand out to stop him.

"Ya see Leon," Ferguson said. "That's why Silas and me came out today. Mr. Kraft had a feeling you wouldn't be reasonable."

Leon pushed at Ferguson's arm. "Get your God damned hands off me!" he growled. He shook his head and then raised an accusing finger up to the Sheriff. "I know what this is," he said. "It's a God damned shakedown!"

"Leon..." Ferguson started.

"You want money? Is that it?" Leon demanded, looking at Ferguson and then the Bureau man. "Well you can't draw blood from a stone Ferguson!"

The two men were face to face, only about a foot apart. "Watch what you're implying there Leon," Ferguson said.

Leon stared hard at Ferguson. "I'm not implying anything Sheriff," he hissed. "Everybody knows what you're about."

Ferguson grimaced and shook his head. "Careful Leon..."

Leon wasn't finished. "You're just a crook with a badge!" he growled.

Ferguson had heard enough. He raised his right hand

and shoved Leon hard in the chest. Leon stumbled backward and then righted himself. He started to step towards Ferguson but stopped suddenly. His face went slack and his eyes lost focus. He opened his mouth but could only let out a gurgling sound.

"Pop!" Jacob shouted.

"Jesus, Leon," Ferguson held his hands up. "I barely touched you."

In his periphery Adam saw a sudden movement. When he turned his head he saw his Uncle Willie coming up from the house. Just as Willie was passing the Sheriff's car, Silas Ferguson caught him by the collar of his coat and spun him into the hood of the car. Willie reached down for the hilt of his hunting knife but before he could reach it Silas, who had drawn his Colt .45 when the fracas had begun, cracked Willie over the back of the head with the butt. Willie crumpled to the ground. Leon mumbled something unintelligible and took a step towards Willie and Silas but his legs gave out and he collapsed.

Adam was frozen where he stood. He looked from his grandfather to his uncle. He was suddenly aware that his father was speaking to him.

"Adam... Adam!" Jacob waited until he was sure he had his son's attention and then said. "Go tell Grandma to call for a doctor! Grandpa is sick."

CHAPTER 10

Adam returned from the dairy barn with Iris a few minutes later. When they arrived Jacob was attending to the still prostrate Leon. Hal had helped Willie over to the pump where he was applying a damp cloth to the back of Willie's head. Maureen had been instructed to go to the house and call Dr. Pritchard in Cattaraugus and have him come out.

Iris surveyed the scene with her brow furrowed. She turned to Sheriff Ferguson who stood with his thumbs hooked in his belt. "What did you do to him?" she snapped.

Ferguson shook his head. "Barely laid a hand on him Iris," he said. "Leon just started sputterin' and then he collapsed.

Iris rushed over to her husband and knelt down. Leon's face had lost all its color and his eyes were opened but unfocused. She looked up at Jacob. "What happened?" She asked.

"The Bureau man said the cows are sick and the milk's bad..."

"What?" Iris cut him off.

"Ma, they said it's the whole herd. They told dad he

had to destroy every head. Dad got agitated and then he just collapsed."

Iris gestured over to her shoulder and spoke in a lower tone, "What about Willie?"

"He came running up and Silas clocked him," Jacob replied.

Iris closed her eyes briefly and then stood up. "Hal!" she barked. "Help Jacob get Leon into the house."

Hal stood up and had Willie put his own hand over the compress. He ambled over to Leon and he and Jacob started to pick the old man up. Willie was regaining his faculties. He stood with the cloth pressed to his head and glared at Silas Ferguson. Silas took notice and then glared back at Willie until Willie broke eye contact and looked down at the ground.

"Iris, I'm sorry," Sheriff Ferguson said. "Just doin' my job." Iris looked at him with her cold gray eyes. The corners of her mouth tightened and then she turned and followed the men into the house.

Leon was taken up to his bed and a few minutes later Iris, Jacob and Hal came back downstairs. Adam and Maureen looked at Jacob expectantly. Willie had disappeared, probably to lick his wounds. Jacob looked glum, his eyes downcast.

"How is he?" Maureen asked.

"He'll be fine," Iris said flatly. "Doc Crandall will be here within the hour.

"Would you like me to wait with you?" Maureen asked. She moved her hand towards her apron pocket, where Adam knew she kept a rosary, one of the few remnants she kept from her Catholic upbringing.

"And do what?" Iris glared at her. "There's work to do. The cows still need to be looked after even if we can't sell the milk and the fields still need to be worked on."

Maureen shook her head but said nothing. Jacob looked at her sympathetically.

"We've already lost an hour of daylight," Iris continued. "There's no sense all of us standing around doing nothing."

Jacob took Maureen by the arm and led her and Adam out of the house.

A steady rain had started falling, big fat cold drops. The field quickly turned into a quagmire. At one point the tractor got stuck and it took all the men to free it. Hal asked if Adam could drive it since he was the smallest but he blanched at the idea and Jacob said he wasn't ready. The work was excruciatingly slow and before they knew it the gray sky turned even darker as evening approached. The work party returned to the barn with sodden clothes and mud caked shoes.

Maureen was waiting for them on the porch. Even though it was damp and cold she had decided to wait outside rather than expose herself to her mother-in-law's contempt any longer than she had to. She took off Adam's hat and started to peel off his coat.

"You'll catch your death of cold," she said.

Adam was embarrassed. He realized that he was supposed to be acting like a man, not a child. And here his mother was treating him like a little boy.

"I'm fine," he said.

Hal and the other hands had returned to the bunk house. Muddy shoes were left on the porch and the family went inside. Iris was making her way down the stairs carrying a tray with a bowl and a cup on it. She looked at her drenched family and snapped, "Get out of those wet clothes and don't make a mess. There's soup in the kitchen."

Dinner was eaten in silence. Adam devoured his soup and bread like it was his last meal. He finally started to feel the chill leave his body. Iris returned to the kitchen just as they were finishing.

"How's pop?" Jacob asked.

Iris wiped her hands on her apron as she returned to the stove. "Doc says he had a stroke," she replied. She started cleaning up and offered nothing else as far as an explanation.

Adam looked at his parents. Maureen had apparently prepared herself for an encounter with her mother-in-law; with a placid look on her face she began to clear the table. Jacob, however, needed to know more.

"A stroke?" he said. "Jesus Ma, how bad is it?"

Iris was carrying the empty soup pot to the wash basin. "We won't know for a while," she replied evenly. "Doc says it's too soon to tell.

Jacob seemed to ponder that for a moment. Then he looked at his mother. "Will he get better?"

Iris had heard enough. She straightened up and turned

towards Jacob, her gray eyes looking hard at him. "I don't know," she said with her voice rising. "I don't know. But we have work to do so I suggest the three of you go home and get some rest. Tomorrow we have to make up for lost time."

Jacob took the hint and gathered Adam and Maureen and left for their house. As they were leaving they saw Willie making his way towards the house. He still had an angry look on his face.

^^^

The next morning Jacob, Maureen and Adam made the trek to his parents' house just after sunrise. The sky had cleared but the air had cooled considerably. It was just above freezing. When they arrived Hal and the other farm hands were standing in front of the house. Hal looked towards Jacob as they walked up with a concerned look on his face.

"What's happening Hal?" Jacob asked.

"Your mother wants a word with us before we get started," Hal replied.

Just then Iris walked out onto the front porch. If she was feeling anything she didn't show it. She had her usual serious demeanor. Willie was a step behind her, he on the other hand seemed to have regained the confidence that had been knocked out of him the day before by Silas Ferguson.

Iris looked down at the assembled family and employees. "Jim, Carl," she said to two of the hands. "You two go with Willie to the dairy barn today." She turned towards Maureen and said, You'll help the men turning over the field."

No one moved or spoke for a moment and then Jacob finally asked, "What's going on? Where is dad?"

Iris glared at him. "Your father will be laid up for a while so we'll just have to make do without him."

"What's going on with the herd?" Jacob pressed on. "What does Willie need Jim and Carl for?"

Adam knew his father wanted to know why Maureen was being forced to work in the field but didn't dare incur Iris' ire by asking it directly.

Iris held her stare at Jacob and said, "We can't sell the milk. We're going to butcher them and sell the meat."

She let that sink in for a moment and then started to say, "We're burning daylight..."

"The whole herd?" Hal interrupted her.

She looked at him directly with her cold, gray stare. "Yes, Hal," she snapped. "The whole herd."

"Beggin' your pardon Ma'am," Hal said looking right back at her. "Is this Mr. Avery's Idea?"

Iris flashed an angry look at the foreman. "Mr. Avery is incapacitated at the moment. And the whole dairy enterprise has just gone up in smoke.   I'm not going to waste any more time or money feeding a bunch of useless animals!"

"But shouldn't we wait until your husband..." Hal started to say.

"God damn it!" Iris cut him off. "If and when Leon is better you can take it up with him. But for now you'll do as I say! Ferguson will be back sooner rather than later and he'll have the State Police with him and those cows will be gone. Do you hear me?"

Hal's face had turned red and he looked down. No one said a word for a moment and then Iris yelled, "Well, what are you waiting for? Get to work!"

CHAPTER 11

Leon's recovery looked like it was going to be long and difficult. Adam would always remember the first time he saw his grandfather two days after the stroke. Leon was sitting in the parlor when the family came in from the fields in the evening. The left side of his face was drooping and his left arm was hanging stiffly at his side. He didn't look at anyone directly or speak. He seemed simultaneously angry and humbled by his plight. The only thing that remained the same was the whiskey glass in his good right hand. Adam overheard Iris telling Jacob the only reason Leon had gotten out of bed was to slake his thirst. It didn't seem to phase her that her husband was doing exactly what the doctor had told him he had to stop doing. When Jacob asked her about it she just shot him a look and said, "He never stopped for anything else, his family, his farm, his health, prohibition... he's not going to stop now."

Sheriff Ferguson did return, this time with three armed deputies. He inquired about the herd and was told that it was being taken care and that the milk from the cows that had yet to be slaughtered was being dumped out as soon as it was extracted.

In reality Iris' plan to sell the meat was a middling success. Willie, for his part, attacked the project with zeal. He was killing and butchering three cows a day. Charlie was the only other farm hand that didn't seem to be phased by the carnage. Lem and Walter had begged off the detail and Hal had flat refused to take part at all.

During a break out in the fields later that week, Adam had heard Hal the foreman talking to Jacob when he thought no one was within earshot. "There has to be another way," Hal had protested. "If the Farm Bureau gets wind of this there'll be trouble."

"I'm thinking after they have a few carcasses go bad Ma will come to her senses," Jacob had responded.

One day Willie and Charlie set off in the truck with a load of meat to try and sell it in a few of the surrounding towns. They managed to sell some but came back with more than half of what they had started with.

"You'll just have to go out again tomorrow," Iris had said flatly.

"I don't know if the meat will keep..." Charlie the field hand had started to say.

Iris shot him a cold stare. "You leave the thinking to us," she said, effectively putting the matter to rest.

It was a dry spring and early summer didn't offer much relief. Jacob fretted to Maureen that the corn wasn't growing and was starting to show signs of dry rot. The family and the workers did what they could but they were up against Mother Nature, a fickle entity at best.

On one particularly hot July day a letter came in the mail. Iris brought it out to where the crew was taking their lunch.

"The price of lumber hit rock bottom and John's uncle is closing the saw mill," Iris told Jacob. "Your sister Constance is coming home."

Jacob had told Adam about how shortly after he enlisted in the army, his sister Connie had married a man named John Tyler and moved to Jamestown where John had a job in his family's mill. Connie had met John when he was in Cattaraugus buying timber. Jacob had told him that Iris hadn't approved of John, something about his character, but Connie was just as headstrong as Iris and moved away without her parents' blessing. They had a daughter, Billie Jean, who was just a few months older than Adam.

"I'm sure you'll be glad to have her back," Maureen offered tentatively.

Iris frowned. "Well there'll be three more mouths to feed," she said. She looked over to where the hired help was laying in the shade. "We may have to let some of the men go."

"Jesus Ma," Jacob said. "Some of the men have been here since I was a kid. Hal's been here longer than I can re-member."

"You don't understand," Iris offered. "We have to take care of the family first. No one else will. Not Hal, not those lay-abouts, not even God."

Maureen looked mortified but held her tongue. Iris turned around and made her way back to the house.

^^^

A few weeks later an old car pulled up the long drive just as the work party was returning to the barn. Jacob put his hand on Adam's shoulder and stood and watched as it pulled up and stopped. John and Connie got out first. John was a good looking man, tall and a little on the heavy side with brown eyes and hair peeking from under his hat. Connie bore a resemblance to her mother Iris, tall and thin, blonde hair and gray eyes but without the coldness that Iris seemed to radiate. Jacob hugged his sister and shook John's hand. He introduced Adam and then Billie walked up next to her mother. Billie was almost fourteen and took after her father as far as her features. She had long brown hair and soft brown eyes.

"This is your cousin Adam sweetheart," Connie said to Billie.

"Hello," Billie said.

Adam tried to respond but couldn't seem to speak. He nodded and said nothing.

John stepped forward and offered his hand to Jacob. "Hello Jake. Connie's told me a lot about you," he said with a broad smile.

"Nice to finally meet you John," Jacob responded, shaking John's hand enthusiastically.

Connie had a concerned look on her face. "Where's dad?" she asked after nodding a few clipped hellos.

"He's in the parlor," Iris' voice cut in. No one had noticed her come out of the house but there she stood on the porch, not a trace of emotion on her face. Connie looked up at her mother and then walked briskly up the steps and went into the house.

John had removed his hat. "Hello Mrs. Avery," he said tentatively.

Iris simply nodded. "Jacob, why don't you and Adam help John take their bags up to Connie's room?" She looked at Billie and a slight smile finally crossed her face. She descended the steps into the yard and offered her hand to her granddaughter. "And you young lady, come to the kitchen with me and tell me about your trip."

Billie looked at her father quizzically. Had John or Connie explained the familial tension caused by their marriage? John nodded at Billie who then smiled demurely at Iris and took her hand.

Adam couldn't understand it completely but his face felt hot. The fact that he felt himself blushing coupled with the fact that he had been tongue-tied in front of his cousin only made him feel more embarrassed. He put his head down and followed his father and Uncle John to the rear of the car to retrieve the bags.

^^^

What should have been a joyous welcome home dinner somehow was a quiet, stilted reunion. John explained how the financing for new buildings had dried up and with it the demand for lumber. John said his uncle, whose health was in decline, decided he had had enough. He took what he had saved and closed the mill before it went under. John had pleaded with him to try to stick it out, but the old man claimed that he had heard that things "...were going to get worse before they got better." He had made up his mind. He was tired and ill and didn't think he would live long enough to see it through.

Iris seemed to listen impassively. Adam thought he noticed an occasional frown across her face as John told his story.

"It's the damned banks!" Leon burst out at one point. "They hold all the cards," he slurred. "They loan money and they charge their interest and when they feel like it they call in the loans and foreclose. They manipulate, they lie... God damned parasites!"

Leon's outburst brought all conversation to a halt. Having made his point, he fell quiet and looked down. He picked up his glass and took a long drink.

CHAPTER 12

Iris wasted little time in following through with her threat of thinning out the help. Willie claimed that he had found a tin of biscuits under Fred's bunk that Iris had said had gone missing. Fred, a quiet and shy young man who had only been with the Averys for a year, had offered little defense besides saying he didn't know how they got there and was let go. Adam had overheard Hal telling Jacob that he didn't think that Fred had thieving in him.

A few weeks later Charlie and Willie got into an argument in their improvised slaughterhouse. No one knew what exactly transpired but when everyone came in from the fields they were told that Iris had told Charlie to pack his things and clear off.

Adam overheard his father and Hal the foreman talking about Charlie. "I don't get it," Hal had said. "Charlie is the easiest going guy I know."

Jacob was just listening without a reply. Hal seemed to sense that the decision had been made and let it go.

Connie and her family tried to settle into the routine

of life on the farm. Connie seemed to have it in her blood. She was equally able in the field, the kitchen or anywhere else she was needed. Billie would mostly shadow her mother and seemed eager to help. John, on the other hand, seemed to be put out by the early mornings and long hours. After Fred and Charlie were dismissed, the demands that Connie and Iris put on him only increased and it didn't seem to sit well with him.

One positive aspect of having Connie and her family back on the farm was that she seemed to form a bond with Maureen. She would often come to visit and help Maureen with the mending.. They would talk as they worked and for the first time since they had arrived at the Hollow Adam thought his mother felt some form of acceptance.

^^^

July came and with it an extended dry spell. Jacob told Adam that the corn was stunted, it should have been 'knee high by the Fourth of July.' If it didn't rain soon the crop would be in jeopardy. The dairy herd had all been slaughtered. Most of the meat had gone bad and had to be burned to cut down on the flies and the stench that had taken over the dairy barn. Iris had more than once referred to the now defunct dairy operation as "Father's Folly." Leon was more sullen than ever.

Adam got over his initial shyness with Billie and they spent much of their free time together, exploring the area around the properties. Adam had known girls from school back in Buffalo, but Billie was different. She was opinionated and insightful, she seemed mature for her age. She told him about growing up in Jamestown and hinted that things didn't exactly happen at the mill the way her father John had described them. When Adam asked for an explanation she would change the subject. He let the topic drop after that. He didn't want to offend the only friend he had. Jacob had become immersed in helping Iris run the farm and had less time to spend with Adam. Jacob had also assumed the role of peacemaker between Iris and Leon as well as Iris and Hal and Iris and John. It was a full time job.

Another thing about Billie that both impressed and embarrassed Adam was that she was allowed to drive the tractor. John had volunteered her, explaining that she had driven his car around the lumber yard back in Jamestown. She was thirteen, a year and a half older than Adam, but to him it seemed like she was much closer to adulthood than he was.

^^^

Life in the Hollow was virtually self-contained. The family grew food to sell as well as to feed themselves. The only exposure to the outside world the family had was when they sold their crops and milk and when they bought supplies in nearby Cattaraugus. That and Leon's dealings with the bank. It was through the bank that the first rumbling came regarding the calamity that was about to transpire all across the country. Letters were sent, telling Leon that the bank was calling in his loans on the equipment he had purchased for the dairy operation. Each one carried a more threatening and ominous tone. The price of corn was at an all-time high and none of the markets were looking to buy much for fear that they would overextend themselves. The harvest had started dubiously as it was, the dry summer had affected the yield and the quality. "Mostly feed corn," Hal had told Adam.

September came and the subject of school for Billie and Adam was never mentioned. Adam knew his mother had reluctantly accepted it. She had been able to pick up a few more dog eared school texts and a copy of *The Adventures of Huckleberry Finn.* Adam devoured this Mark Twain novel as eagerly as he had the first. Adam asked Billie if her parents were concerned about her missing school. "Mother says there is enough to learn here," Billie had replied.

Then one day in late October Adam's uncle John brought a newspaper home from a trip into town and the family gathered in the parlor as he read from it. Adam heard words and concepts he didn't understand like "Stock Market and Default," but all the same he knew it was serious by the expressions on the faces of his family. After a while Iris snapped at Maureen, "Take the children outside. We need to discuss things. Adam shot his mother a glance. She just nodded and ushered Billie and Adam out through the front door. The three of them sat on the porch on a chill October day and Maureen tried to engage them in small talk. Moments later they heard voices being raised, the words were inaudible but the emotion was clear. Something unpleasant was about to happen.

After a while Jacob came out, red-faced. He glanced at his family, unable to mask his anger. Maureen stood up and went to him, placing her hand on his arm. "Are you alright?" she asked.

"As alright as I can be," he replied. "I have to go to the bunk house and tell Hal and the Lem they're being let go." Without waiting for a response he put his hat on and walked off the porch towards the bunk house.

^^^

Sunday dinner was a grim affair that week. Adam could feel the tension in his grandparents' house as soon as they arrived. Leon was already in his cups. He sat at the head of the table sullenly, the left side of his face seemed more slack than usual. It was mostly silent during the meal, Connie and Maureen tried to initiate a conversation but eventually gave in to the prevailing mood.

As the dishes were being cleared John spoke up. "Pop," he said to Leon. "I was wondering if we could have a word?"

Iris stopped what she was doing and looked at John. "And what would that be?" she asked with a bit of an edge.

John tightened the corners of his mouth. "I think I have a way to make some money."

Iris scoffed and said, "We're all ears John."

John blushed slightly. "Well... it's just..." he looked around the table.

Iris seemingly understood. She frowned and said, "Constance, Maureen, Billie, you girls see to the dishes." She looked at Adam and then said, "Adam, help your Uncle Willie bring in some firewood from the shed," then back at John, "We'll go talk in the parlor."

"Ma?" Willie started. Obviously he felt slighted by not being included in the adult's conversation. Whatever he was going to ask, Iris closed him off with a look from her cool gray eyes.

Adam moved quickly with his chore. On the one hand, the less time he spent alone with Willie the better. He also was deeply curious what his Uncle John's plan was. He went to the shed silently behind Willie and collected an armload of wood. To Adam's relief, Willie seemed to be in a hurry as well; he moved quickly back towards the house without saying a word or even acknowledging his nephew. Willie climbed the porch stairs and set his bundle down silently. He turned to Adam, glared at him and put a finger to his lips. Adam set his load down as quietly as possible and they crept over to the parlor window which was propped slightly open.

"We have almost everything we need," John was saying. "We can use the milk cans for collection and all the tubes and line for the condenser."

"Have you ever done it?" Leon slurred. "Do you know how?"

"More likely to blow himself up," Iris said.

"I've seen it done!" John protested. "Pop, how much do you pay for the rotgut you get from Stevenson?"

"Two bucks a bottle."

"And it costs him pennies to make." Adam had yet hear to John so animated. "There's a market. I have connections in Jamestown. Pop, you said yourself that the Volstead Act is a violation of our..."

"Never mind that!" Iris interrupted. "Leave that to the politicians. Don't try to sell this as something it's not."

"Not to mention it's still illegal," Jacob added. "We've already got the Sheriff breathing down our necks."

"That crook!" Leon erupted. "Stevenson pays him off every month to look the other way."

The room fell silent. Adam and Willie looked at each other wondering if they had been discovered eavesdropping. Adam was about to bolt when Iris spoke up. "We'll do it," she said. "On two conditions. One, you do it someplace where if you do blow yourself up no one will notice. Two, you run the still but Jacob runs the business end of it. Understood?"

"Well," John said quietly. "I think I..."

"I don't care what you think!" Iris interrupted. "If we're going to do this we're going to do it right, and that means Jacob is in charge."

"Okay," John said meekly.

A moment of silence was followed by the sound of Iris' voice. "Just how long does it take to fetch a few logs?" Willie and Adam looked at each other again and then backed away from the window.

^^^

As it turned out John had a talent for producing moonshine. After a few weeks and only a handful of misfires, he had a few dozen bottles ready to take down to his connection in Jamestown. The carburetor in his car was malfunctioning so it was decided they would take the truck. Jacob and John loaded up the truck at dusk and started on their way.

They made a left onto Windmill Road and were headed towards Route 242 and Jamestown. A mile from the junction they rounded a bend and found a car blocking the two lane road. There was lettering on the side that said *Cattaraugus County Sheriff* and a lone figure was leaning on the fender. As they pulled closer the lights revealed that it was Deputy Silas Ferguson and he was holding a shotgun over his shoulder. Ferguson raised himself off the fender and strolled up to the driver's side window.

"Evening Jake," he drawled. He bent closer to look across at the passenger seat. "You must be Connie's husband," he said to John.

Jacob glanced at John, who just nodded, his face ashen.

"You're a lucky man," Ferguson continued. "Half the county had a thing for Jake's sister back in the day."

"What can we do for you Silas?" Jacob asked.

"Well, it's a funny thing," Ferguson said straightening up. "I heard a rumor that there was contraband liquor being run through our county roads and I didn't believe it." He let that hang in the air for a moment and then gestured towards the back of the truck. "I know you're not delivering milk anymore, especially this time of night. So I'm curious as to what you would be transporting under the tarp?"

Jacob smiled and opened the door. Ferguson took a step back and brought the shotgun off his shoulder. Jacob put his hands up and said, "Easy Silas."

Ferguson relaxed and smiled back. "Can't be too careful Jake, there's a lot of desperate people these days."

"Don't I know it," Jacob said. He walked to the back of the truck and undid the rope that was securing the tarp. "I know you know what this is," he said as he pulled back the tarp revealing the wooden crates underneath.

Ferguson clucked his tongue and looked at the crates. John had also gotten out of the cab and was looking on anxiously. Ferguson tapped one of the crates with the barrel of the shotgun, looked at John and said, "Open it."

John looked at Jacob who nodded his ascent and then went back to the cab and came back with a pry bar, Ferguson had stepped back out of arm's reach and watched as John pried open the crate. "Step back," he said to John, who obliged immediately. Ferguson stepped back up to the truck and removed a bottle from the crate.

"Oh my," Ferguson said. "You boys may be in some trouble." He looked from Jacob to John.

"How much?" Jacob asked flatly.

"Excuse me?" Ferguson asked with seemingly exaggerated surprise.

"How does this work?" Jacob continued. "I know you and your daddy get a cut from the others. How much do you need?"

Ferguson frowned. "Are you trying to bribe a sworn officer of the law?" he asked.

Jacob closed his eyes, exhaled and then said, "I'd call it more of a business arrangement."

Ferguson laughed. "Always the smart one weren't you." he looked at the bottle for a moment and then said, "Twenty percent of what you sell."

"What?" John erupted. "Leon was right! You guys are the real crooks!"

Ferguson shot John an evil look and with one hand, leveled the shotgun in his direction. "You better tell your brother-in-law to mind his manners Jake."

"Get back in the truck John," Jacob said.

John's expression had gone from outrage to terror. He grimaced and turned to go back to the passenger side of the truck.

"Twenty percent then," Jacob said to Ferguson. "And you can keep that bottle as a gift."

"I was going to anyway, but thanks," Ferguson sneered. He turned to walk back towards his car. "You boys have a good night," he said over his shoulder.

And so it went, as long as the Averys made a regular payment to Deputy Ferguson the Sheriff's department let them run their liquor to Jamestown. John was able to increase the production as he went along and with the meager income the farm pulled in the family was able to satisfy the loan payments. The Averys survived that way for the next two years until the night Silas Ferguson murdered Jacob in cold blood.

PART TWO

CHAPTER 13

February 1932

Two days after Jacob's burial Willie and John brought the truck over to collect Maureen and Adam and their things. Adam could tell his mother was broken-hearted. Even though the house was still a humble three room structure with no electricity or running water, his parents had made it into a comfortable home. Iris had already spoken as to their accommodations. Maureen would be staying with Billie in Willie's old room and Adam would be staying with his Uncle Willie in the now empty bunk house. Adam felt sick to his stomach at the thought of being in that close proximity to Willie but he put on a brave face for his mother, who he knew had enough on her mind already.

The first night in the bunkhouse Adam had gone to bed while Willie was still up at the house. He was wide awake lying on the Spartan cot that would be his for the foreseeable future pretending to be asleep. Willie came in a short time later and Adam squeezed his eyes shut and tried to control his breathing. He was at least grateful when he heard Willie open the wood stove and place a couple of logs into it, the bunkhouse was drafty and dank. When he heard Willie walk over to his own bunk he opened his eyes a sliver and looked at his uncle. Willie had removed his shirt and Adam almost gasped audibly. There were long, red scars angled across Willie's back. It looked as though they had been there a while but they were still notice-able. It was all Adam could do to shut his eyes again as Willie put on a nightshirt and turned down the lamp. Eventually, fatigue took over and Adam drifted off into a fitful sleep. That night he would dream about fire and loss.

The next thing he knew he, Willie was poking him on the shoulder. Adam opened his eyes and saw Willie standing over him with the lamp. It was still dark outside so Adam had no idea what time it was. He stared up at Willie, struggling to imagine what he wanted.

"C'mon, get up," Willie said. "Time to go to work."

The family gathered for a solemn breakfast. Adam still couldn't believe that he would never see his father again. He was still in shock and too terrified to tell anyone what he had witnessed outside the shed the night Silas Ferguson killed his father. He was convinced that if he told anyone, Ferguson would come back and kill him too.

The next few months were busier than the past few winters. With the help run off and Leon incapacitated, there were fewer people to get the farm and all the equipment ready for planting season. Adam withdrew into himself. It was hard to talk to his mother since privacy was at a minimum. His few interactions with his cousin Billie seemed awkward and stilted now. The farm and the family seemed to be living under the cloud of Jacob's death with no relief in sight.

Spring came and the planting was begun. The days were long and despite an average snowfall, the ground was still dry from the previous summer. The whole family was turned out to work the fields now with the exception of Leon, who would make an occasional appearance, seemingly just to scowl and mutter oaths under his breath.

Billie and Adam eventually resumed a more cordial relationship. What little free time they had they spent together, wandering the outskirts of the farm or going to the creek that ran between the Avery's property and the land formerly occupied by Adam's family. One particularly humid Sunday in early July they found themselves down by the creek.

"You don't like it here very much do you?" Billie asked Adam.

Adam looked at his cousin, wondering why she would ask. "I dunno... do you?" he responded.

She looked right back at him with her earnest brown eyes. "I hate it," she said. "I miss my friends and our house in Jamestown." She stated to remove her boots. "Do you miss Buffalo?"

"Yeah," Adam said, looking down at the ground. "Sort of. We had to leave though."

"I know," Billie said surprising him.

Adam looked at her. As she was peeling off her socks she noticed and said, "Momma told me about the trouble that your dad had there."

Jacob fell silent. His family's departure from Buffalo would always be a painful memory for him, the fear the anger and the feeling of helplessness that his parents had tried unsuccessfully to hide for his benefit. He often wondered how things would have been different if they had settled anywhere else than The Hollow.

Billie stopped what she was doing, noticing Adam's discomfort. "It's okay," she said. "We had to leave our home too."

"Because the mill closed?"

Billie smiled wanly and shook her head. "That's only part of the story," she said. She took a step into the part of the creek where the water collected at a bend and winced. "Oh my gosh, it's cold." She took a step farther out and turned back towards Adam. "Poppa got caught stealing from his uncle," she said. "The mill was closing anyway but he was in trouble with his family. They threatened to have him put in jail."

Adam was struck by Billie's candor, matter of fact, admitting that her father was something other than what he claimed to be. He stood just looking at Billie not knowing what to say. "You should come in," Billie said.

"You said it was cold," Adam replied.

"Yeah but it feels good." With that Billie kicked her foot in Adam's direction splashing water on his legs. "C'mon, don't be a sissy," she added. Then without warning she lifted off her dress and tossed it on the bank. The water was only a few feet deep but she laid down in it and pushed herself into the center of the pool. Adam stood motionless, not knowing what to do.

When Billie stood up her wet undergarments were clinging to her skin. Adam felt himself blush and turned away.

Billie laughed and said, "Your loss, this feels so good." Adam heard her splash again and glanced back in her direction. She emerged from the water and collected her dress. "I didn't mean to embarrass you," she said. Adam turned to face her. She was dripping wet but now holding her dress in front of her. She looked at him earnestly with her long hair falling over her shoulders.

"It's okay," he said quietly. He turned while she pulled the dress on over her head and pulled it down.

"I feel bad for you and your mom then," Adam said, eager to change the subject.

"Well don't," Billie said flatly. "Momma's no angel either."

CHAPTER 14

By mid-July it was obvious that the crop yield was going to be dismal again that year. No one discussed it but there was a sense of dread hanging over the farm. Adam and Willie had settled into a peaceful coexistence; Adam was deferential to his uncle and minded his own business. His curiosity about the marks on Willie's back went unanswered. Maureen was doing her best to keep up appearances. Adam asked Billie how she thought Maureen was doing and Billie replied, "She's quiet, but she seems okay. She's tougher than you think."

One muggy morning as the family was getting ready to head out to the fields, a battered truck pulled up the drive to the front of the house. Iris stood on the top step of the porch with her arms folded across her chest. There were three children in the back of the truck. Adam figured they had to be between ten and six years old. The driver's side door opened and a thin, shabbily dressed man got out. He removed his hat and walked up to the bottom of the porch steps.

"Good morning Ma'am," he said to Iris.

"Good morning," Iris replied warily.

The man gestured back to the truck and said, "I've been out of work for some time and my family and myself were checking the local farms to see if there might be some work."

Iris frowned slightly. "I'm sorry," she said. "With the state of our crop we're barely going to have enough to feed ourselves."

"I understand," the man said quickly. "We're working our way up to Axeville to pick strawberries." He bowed slightly and added, "But thank you for your time and God bless." He turned to return to his family when Iris spoke up.

"Wait a moment," she said. The man turned around and looked up at her. "Your children must be hungry. There's oatmeal left on the stove. Why don't you bring them in and we'll put some food into them. And you're welcome to take all the water you need from the well."

The man's mouth moved but nothing came out right away. He wrung the brim of his hat in his hands and then glanced back at his wife in the truck. He turned back to Iris, looking like he was about to cry and said, "God bless you ma'am . . . that would be wonderful."

"Go ahead then, bring them in," Iris said with uncharacteristic warmth. She looked across the yard to where Willie was standing. "Willie, I need to speak to you for a moment." Willie obediently scuttled over to the porch steps and followed his mother into the house.

They had only been at work in the fields for about an hour, weeding and checking the stalks for insects when Willie came rushing up to where they were working. Everyone stopped what they were doing and looked at him. Willie always seemed self-conscious, now with everyone staring at him it seemed to be worse.

"Momma... wants everyone... to come back to the house," he stammered, looking down at his feet.

"Why?" John snapped. He was always irritable when doing manual labor.

"John!" Connie raised her voice. "It must be important if she's calling us in."

John still looked irritated but he didn't say another word. With the issue resolved the family gathered up their tools and started back towards the house. Adam was lost in thought at the tail end of the procession when suddenly Willie grabbed him by the arm and looked him in the eye.

"Ma says you need to go to the bunk house and get six bedrolls and put them in the truck."

Adam looked at Willie dumbfounded. Willie squeezed his arm and hissed "Go on, do it!"

When Adam had done as he was told and returned to the house he was met by Willie, who came flying out of the front door. Willie's cheeks were flushed and when he saw Adam he snapped at him, "Go back and get a change of clothes."

Once again Adam froze, trying to grasp what was happening and why Willie looked so upset.

"Get goin'!" Willie barked.

Adam went back to the bunkhouse and stuffed a change

of clothes into an old knapsack that one of the workers had left
behind and returned to the house. Most of the family was loading their things into the truck except for Leon and Maureen,
who were standing on the porch watching. When Maureen saw
Adam she walked quickly down the steps and rushed over to
him, glancing over her shoulder once in Iris' direction.

"Adam," Maureen said putting her hands on his shoulders. Adam had undergone a growth spurt in the recent
months and they now stood almost eye to eye. "You're going to
be going away for a few days with your Grandmother and aunt
and uncles..."

"Where?" Adam asked.

"Your Grandmother got the idea from that family that
stopped by this morning that we could make money working on
other people's farms."

Adam glanced over at the truck. Uncle John was behind the
wheel, turning the engine over. Iris was giving instructions to
Willie and Aunt Connie. Billie was already sitting in the back
looking like she couldn't care less. Suddenly, something occurred to him.

"You said 'I' have to go with them. Aren't you coming?"

"She told me I was to stay behind and look after Leon,"
Maureen replied.

Adam looked after his mother without knowing what to
say.

"Adam!" Iris' voice cut in. "It's time to go."

Adam looked at his mother, but he couldn't read her expression. Then she pulled him close and whispered to him, "Stay close to Billie, she'll watch out for you."

Adam was distraught at having to go with his family without his mother. At the same time he was slightly embarrassed that his mother had asked his cousin to look after him, she was less than a year older than he was. With a jumble of emotions he pulled away from his mother and walked towards the truck.

They'd been heading north towards Axeville for around twenty minutes. Adam was lost in thought and barely noticed the truck slowing down. From his seat in the bed of the truck next to Billie he looked through the cab and saw another, older truck off to the side of the road ahead. John was slowing down and as they got closer Adam could see that it was the family that had come to the Hollow that morning looking for work. The mother and children were standing off to the side and the father must have been under the open hood at the front of the truck. Through the window Adam saw Iris say something to John who shot her an incredulous look and then accelerated again, passing by the broken down truck without even another glance. Adam thought that the other family was having some of the worst luck possible until he saw his Uncle Willie barely able to hide a wicked smile.

CHAPTER 15

Forty minutes and a few turns later, the truck slowed again, this time turning onto a gravel driveway surrounded on both sides by a whitewashed split rail fence. No one had said a word after passing the family in the disabled vehicle and the mood in the back of the truck was somber. As they pulled up the drive and past a few oak trees a large house came into view. It was two stories, painted white with a wraparound porch. The sun was shining brightly now and the house seemed to radiate the sun's brilliance. John pulled up near the front of the house and pulled the parking brake. Iris was out of the truck first and walked to the back of the truck. "You two, come with me," she said to Billie and Adam. Adam reluctantly got up and hopped off the back of the truck. They followed Iris up the steps and when she got to the front door she pulled a rope that rang a bell inside the house.

Iris turned around to assess her grandchildren. "Stand up straight," she hissed at Adam.

"May I help you?" said a plump young woman who had appeared in the screen door. She was wearing an apron and a scarf around on her head.

Iris relaxed the muscles on her face and turned back to the door. "Would you be Mrs. Shaw?"

Instead of opening the screen door, she looked them up and down. She then looked over at the truck and the rest of the family. "No," she said flatly. "Mrs. Shaw is inside. I'm the housekeeper." "Actually we were looking for Mr. Shaw," Iris said. "We've come to work." Adam noticed his grandmother had changed her tone slightly when she realized she was dealing with the help.

The housekeeper looked at Iris again somewhat disapprovingly. "I see," she said. "Mr. Shaw can probably be found at the greenhouse at the moment." She made a gesture to the driveway that went past the house back to the fields. "Just follow the drive. You can't miss it." With one more glance at Billie and Adam she turned on her heel and went back into the house.

They climbed back into the truck and John drove past the house. Adam couldn't believe his eyes. The fields of the Shaw farm were immense. Furthermore all the plants that he could see from the truck were healthy and green, unlike the crop back home. The truck slowed again and pulled up to a large building that seemed to be made entirely of glass. A short stocky man emerged from a door in the side of the greenhouse and looked their way. He was wearing a broad brimmed straw hat and despite the heat a vest and starched white shirt. Iris alit from the passenger side door and he looked at her curiously.

"Mr. Shaw?" Iris asked.

"Yes," was all he said. He removed his hat revealing a full head of well-groomed white hair that was matched by a neatly trimmed mustache and eyebrows. He removed a handkerchief from his pocket and mopped his brow.

"I understand you're in need of pickers," Iris pressed on undaunted.

Shaw returned his hat to his head and pursed his lips. He shook his head and said, "I'm afraid you've been misinformed, my dear. We have enough help."

For the first time in Adam's memory, Iris seemed unsure of herself. "Oh..." she uttered.

"As soon as the Webers arrive we'll be full up," Shaw added.

Iris seemed to realize something then. She rediscovered her resolve and took a step towards Shaw. "Oh, didn't you hear?" she asked with her hands clasped in front of her chest.

"Hear what?" Shaw said with a frown.

"Darla... I mean Mrs. Weber has taken ill."

"Ill? With what?" Shaw asked. And then, "Do you know the Webers?"

Iris gave a mournful look and said, "Yes, Marvin Weber and I are first cousins. Poor Darla has tuberculosis I'm afraid. They've quarantined the entire family. She didn't want to leave you in a lurch so she asked if we could come in their place."

Shaw shook his head and said, "TB, how dreadful. Are the children alright?"

"Yes... so far," Iris replied solemnly.

Shaw stared at her appraisingly. "It's not easy work. Have you ever picked before?"

"I've lived on farms my whole life," Iris replied. She glanced over her shoulder at the truck and her family. "We have our own place down near Napoli."

Shaw looked at her perplexedly. "And you don't have enough to do on your own land?" he asked.

Iris looked down at the ground and said quietly, "I'm afraid not. The last two summers have been hard and this year's crop is literally dying in the fields."

Shaw shook his head and pursed his lips again. "I've been telling folk around here to modernize for years," he said. He pointed at the vast field to his right. "Do you see that? It would be dry as a desert if it weren't for the irrigation ditches and the pumps."

Iris looked over at the fields with a hand shielding her eyes from the sun. She looked back at Shaw and said, "We've had a string of bad luck..."

"Nonsense!" Shaw rumbled. This country wouldn't be in the shape it's in if more people used a little foresight."

Iris seemed rebuked. She looked down at her feet again but said nothing. Shaw straightened his vest again. "Very well then. If you're willing to put in the work I think we can fit you people in." He turned towards the door to the greenhouse and yelled, "Albert!"

A moment later a tall gaunt man wearing a pair of dirty overalls and wire rimmed glasses stepped out of the door and

looked from Iris to the truck and then to Shaw. "Yes sir?" he
said with a slight accent.

"Take these people over to the barn and show them
where to put their things," Shaw said.

Albert tipped his dirty cap to Shaw and then started to
walk towards the truck. Iris started to turn but Shaw called out
to her, "Oh... Miss..."

"Johnston," Iris said.

"Yes, Miss Johnston. I take it your cousin explained the
pay structure here?"

Iris seemed caught off guard for a split second and then
recovered. "Of course," she replied.

"And we do have expectations regarding the behavior of
guest workers."

Iris nodded. "Of course," she said with a slight bow of
her head.

"Very well," Shaw added. He removed a watch from his
vest pocket and opened it. "You get settled in and then after
lunch Morris will take you out to the fields and you can get
started." With that he turned and walked back towards the
greenhouse. As Iris turned back towards the truck she scowled
and muttered something under her breath.

Their accommodations were to be in the loft of a newer
barn that was used mostly to house farm equipment. Albert
quietly showed them their spot and explained that there were
only four straw filled mattresses, since they were expecting only
the Webers. "I suppose I could get you a few old feed sacks and

you could make a fifth," he said. He told them that there was no cooking in the loft but they were welcome to use the fire pit outside. Iris had brought a few pots and utensils from her kitchen so she said that would do.

"Whose things are those?" John asked pointing at a few bedrolls and boxes a few feet away from where they were standing.

Albert looked at him for a moment with raised eyebrows and then said, "There's another family, the Jordans. They come every year." He looked around and then added, "I'll meet you by the greenhouse in a half hour and get you started."

"Thank you," Iris said.

As soon as Morris had descended the stairs from the loft and was out of earshot John spoke up, "Sleeping in the barn? Like livestock? And crammed in with a bunch of..."

"Quiet!" Iris snapped. "Do you want your daughter to go hungry?" John opened his mouth but then bit off whatever he was going to say.

Iris glared at him and added, "We took you in when you came crawling back from the mess you made in Jamestown! Now you're going to start paying off your debt."

John's face turned crimson and he looked down at his feet.

Iris smoothed the front of her dress and said, "I brought some sandwiches. Unless anyone else has something to say, I suggest we eat and then get to work."

^^^

After a short time stooped over in the field picking berries in the hot sun, Adam decided that he had finally found something he liked less than picking corn. The family worked their way from one end of one of the larger fields to the other. Their instructions were to pick only the riper berries and then they were to return later in the week and pick the rest. Off in the distance they could see another party in a different field apparently doing the same thing. Occasionally Albert would come out driving a small horse drawn cart with a bucket of water and a tin cup for them. Adam had the feeling that Albert was also checking up on them. He would look into the baskets holding the berries and once had even chastised John for picking berries that weren't ripe yet. Adam watched his uncle John make an obscene gesture at Albert as soon as the man had turned around.

Adam had no concept of the time that they had spent in the field. The sun had moved across the sky but it was still hot and humid. Finally a bell rang off in the distance. Albert approached, on horseback this time, and called out, "That will be all today. Mr. Shaw would like you to come up to the house for dinner."

At the back of the Shaw's house there was a large, makeshift table made up of saw horses and wood planks. The housekeeper was setting the places and Albert was placing chairs around it. Albert looked up and saw the Averys approaching and said, "Ah, good. Please have a seat. Mr. Shaw will be right with you."

Adam counted ten seats at the table. He waited for Iris to make a move and she took a seat near the end of the table. Connie and John sat next to her and then Willie, Billie and Adam sat across from them.

"Evening!" came a voice from their left. Adam looked up and a black man, woman and two children walking towards the table. The man walked up to where John was sitting and extended his hand. "I'm Simon Jordan. This here's my wife Belle and our children Donald and Lucy."

John sat slack-jawed, just staring at Simon Jordan's large calloused hand. Connie took the initiative and stood up pulling John to his feet. "We're the Johnstons, from Napoli," she said. John somewhat reluctantly shook Simon's hand.

"Good!" Ezra Shaw's voice boomed out as he approached the table. "I see everyone's got acquainted. Please have a seat." Shaw then sat down at the end of the table. "Mae!" he bellowed. The back door to the house swung open and the housekeeper emerged carrying a large pot."

"Will Mrs. Shaw be joining us?" Connie asked.

Shaw looked at her blankly for a moment and then said, "I'm afraid Mrs. Shaw is under the weather... the heat I'm afraid."

"I'm sorry to hear that," Connie replied.

John reached out for the ladle that was sticking out of the pot and Iris shot him a scowl. He retracted his hand and looked chastised.

Ezra Shaw bowed his head and everyone at the table

followed suit. "Lord," he began, "Thank you for the food that you have provided us and the work you have given us. May we continue to strive to earn your blessings."

"Amen," the Jordans said in unison.

"Amen," Iris added. Adam glanced at his grandmother. She had a beatific smile on her face, something he'd never seen before.

In between bites of lamb stew and fresh baked bread, Ezra Shaw spent most of the meal talking about how he had foreseen the collapse of the banks coming; "Bad loans, inflated prices . . . avarice and greed are what put his country in the state it's in!" And how he had managed to insulate himself for the coming calamity; "Hard work, planning ahead and most of all not buying the snake oil the crooks in the city were selling!"

The subject of family came up and Shaw shook his head and said, "I'm afraid I have no one to pass this on to. My wife was unable to give me any children."

"That is a shame," Connie said. "Children are a blessing," she added, putting a hand on Billie's arm.

All of it had barely registered with Adam. It was one of the best meals that he had had in a long time. Before he knew it the pot was empty and Shaw stood up. "Very well then," he said, brushing some crumbs off his vest. "I'll see everyone at sunrise."

"Thank you Mr. Shaw," Simon Jordan said rising. "G'night sir." The rest of his family stood up as well and turned to leave.

"Yes, thank you Mr. Shaw," Iris said. "And thank Mae for the delicious meal."

Shaw smiled slightly and said, "That's her job Mrs. Johnston." He then put his hat back on and turned towards the house.

As they walked back to the barn, John was livid. "That pompous ass!" he said. Prattling on about how superior he is to us mere mortals."

Connie put her hand on John's arm and said, "Keep your voice down!"

John shook off her hand and went on, "And we're put out in a barn with a bunch of niggers!"

Iris walked up to John with fire in her eyes and slapped him hard across the face. "I told you, keep your opinions to yourself! If you want this family to eat and have a roof over their head you'll keep your mouth shut and do as you're told."

John was about to reply when he saw Willie with his hand on the hilt of his knife. Iris turned on her heel and headed off to the barn. The rest of them followed without another word.

CHAPTER 16

John slept as far away from everyone as he possibly could that night. Adam was so exhausted he fell asleep immediately and slept straight through the night until a nearby rooster sounded the coming of daybreak. It had rained during the night and the humidity didn't seem as severe as the day before. It was still hot though, and the fields seemed to go on forever.

That afternoon when Albert brought the water cart out to them Connie asked him about his accent. "I am originally from Austria-Hungary," he told her.

"Where's that?" Willie asked.

"It's in Europe," Albert replied. He gave Willie a skeptical look. "That's across the ocean."

"I know where Europe is," Willie said. "My brother was in the war."

"Oh..."

Willie squinted at Albert. "Were you in the war?" he asked.

"Well... yes I was, in a way."

"What does that mean?"

"I was in the signal corps," Albert replied. "I was a messenger."

"You were with the Huns?" Willie asked.

Albert looked at Willie quizzically. He shook his head and said, "It was a long time ago." He then turned and climbed back on the cart.

Three days passed by with the family working from sunrise to just before dusk. It turned out, dinner with Mr. Shaw was a one-time event. The Averys and the Jordans were left to their own devices for their meals. Iris was less than pleased when told if she wanted food from the Shaw's own stores to prepare meals it would come out of their pay. She reluctantly agreed and frugally chose less expensive items, salt pork, beans, turnips. The third night there was a chicken in the pot. It smelled delicious to Adam, especially after the last few days of peasant food. He thought nothing of it until Albert approached them while they were eating. Iris was the first one to look up and notice him. "Did you need something?" she asked flatly.

Albert looked from the pot to Iris with a blank expression. "Excuse me?" he said.

"Are you looking for something?" Iris asked.

Albert shook his head and raised his hand. "No, no, just checking to see if everything was good."

"It's fine," Willie said casting a dirty look at Albert.

"Ya... good. We'll see you in the morning then," Albert said as he turned to leave.

"What was that all about," Connie asked.

"God damned Kraut better mind his own business…" Willie said. He looked down as soon as he saw Iris' withering stare.

At the end of the fourth day Albert tallied the berries they picked and then cleared his throat. "Half day tomorrow," he said. "The fields are clear and we won't be needing your services."

Iris gazed at him. "I thought we'd be here a few more days," she said.

Albert shook his head. "No, the fields are picked clean. We only have enough work for the Jordans."

John made a rude nose with his lips. "Is that right?" he said. "Tossed over for a bunch of darkies."

"John," Connie said sharply. If she was worried about her mother's reaction to John she needn't have been. Iris was focused on Albert. "Why them and not us?" she asked him.

Albert made a show of closing his notebook. He looked at Iris but couldn't maintain eye contact. "You'll have to take that up with Mr. Shaw," he said turning away. He almost walked into Willie who was standing right beside him glaring at him with his deep set eyes. Albert stepped around Willie and walked away quickly.

John knew enough to keep his opinions to himself that night. Barely a word was said at dinner and the Jordan's seemed to pick up on the tension. They kept as far away from the Averys as they could that night.

Out in the fields the next morning Adam thought that

his grandmother had been right; there seemed to be plenty of berries ready to be picked. Something felt off. At noon Albert met them with his notebook in hand and quietly tallied the harvest. "Go and gather your things and then meet Mr. Shaw at the house and he'll settle up with you." He closed the notebook and turned away from Iris' glare.

They gathered their things and loaded up the truck. John pulled up to the house and Iris climbed out and said, "Willie, John, come with me." Willie hopped off the truck quickly and John followed with an unpleasant look on his face. Adam watched as they climbed the porch stairs and knocked on the door. After a moment Mae, the housekeeper opened the door and let them in. Adam, Connie and Billie sat silently in the back of the truck for a few moments until they heard a scream come from inside the house. A chill shot through Adam. Despite his fear, he leapt off the back of the truck and ran towards the house.

"Adam!" his aunt Connie yelled. It was too late though. He took the steps two at a time and burst through the front door. He froze when he saw Ezra Shaw laying on the ground in the parlor with a fresh gash across his temple. Willie was standing over him with a piece of firewood in his hand breathing heavily. Iris was face to face with Mae.

"What have you done?" Mae shrieked.

"Your employer is a cheat and a thief," Iris yelled back.

Mae looked from Iris to Shaw. "What are you talking about?" she asked.

"The work we did?" Iris answered. "Breaking our backs in the fields and sleeping in the barn like a bunch of animals and he pays us pennies?"

Mae shook her head. "No... no... that's the going rate for migrant workers. Albert tallies the pick at the end of the day..."

"Then Albert's a liar!" Iris cut her off.

Mae shook her head once more. "You can't do this," she said. She turned to go to the kitchen. Iris looked at Willie and nodded. Willie quickly set off after Mae. "John!" Iris barked. "Grab the strong box." It was then that she noticed Adam staring at the scene open-mouthed. "What are you doing in here?" she snapped. Adam stood motionless, lost in the surrealness of it all. "Get back to the truck!" Iris snapped. Just as Adam regained his wits and started to turn, a crash came from the kitchen and the sound of a pot being knocked to the floor. "Go!" Iris yelled. Adam turned to leave and noticed her for the first time at the top of the stairs, an old woman in a nightgown, her straggly white hair undone and a horrified confused look on her sunken features. She made eye contact with Adam and then turned and fled back into the upstairs hallway.

As they drove away Adam dared not make eye contact with anyone. He sat with his knees drawn up to his chest. As they neared the bend in the drive he took one last look back at the house and saw smoke pouring out of the first floor windows.

CHAPTER 17

They arrived back in the Hollow late that afternoon. A breeze had picked up offering relief from
the heat. No one had spoken since they left the Shaw farm.
Adam stole glances from time to time at the family members
in the back of the truck. All of them seemed lost in thought
except for Willie. The first part of the journey he was breathing heavily and talking to himself. Later on he calmed down but
took to rocking back and forth where he sat.

They pulled up in front of the house and quietly
climbed off the back of the truck. Adam found himself face to
face with his grandmother. Billie stopped where they were and
looked at Iris.

"Go inside with your mother dear and check on your
grandfather. We'll be right in."

Billie glanced at Adam and then went into the house.
"We need to talk about what happened today Adam," Iris began.

Despite the fact that his mind was racing Adam found
himself unable to speak. He looked down at the ground and felt
nauseous.

"Look at me Adam," Iris said quietly.

Adam was fighting back tears as he looked up at her.

"That man..." she shook her head. "That man was evil. The work we did and the time we spent..." she paused and clenched her fists. "Slave wages! That's what he gave us. I tried to reason with him but he became belligerent and then hostile. And you know your uncle Willie. He's excitable and if nothing else, loyal to this family."

Adam wanted to say something, anything to get away from his grandmother but once again words failed him.

Iris put a hand on his shoulder. It was the first time she had shown any kind of familiarity with him and it only added to his discomfort. "What I need you to promise me is that you won't say anything to your mother just yet. It was a terrible accident and I don't want her to misunderstand it and get upset."

Adam couldn't believe it. He had witnessed Willie cause the death of three people, Shaw, Mae the housekeeper and, in all probability, Mrs. Shaw, and now he was being asked to be silent about it. His stomach churned and he felt light-headed.

"Believe me boy, it's for the best." Iris stared hard into Adam's eyes. "You understand, don't you?"

"Yes ma'am," Adam heard himself say.

They went into the house and found Maureen and Leon in the parlor. Maureen walked up to Adam and threw her arms around him and kissed him on the cheek. Adam felt himself blush, knowing that his grandmother was right behind him, watching him. He pulled away from his mother and looked down at the floor.

"How are you love?" Maureen asked, looking at Adam.

"I'm fine," Adam replied quietly.

"Is everything alright here?" Iris interrupted the reunion.

"As well as can be, Mother Avery," Maureen replied.

"She did fine," Leon slurred. Adam looked at his grandfather. He was freshly shaved and was wearing a clean shirt. Iris looked at Leon skeptically. "Well, I'll get dinner started then," she said. "We can catch up then." With that she shot Adam one more knowing glance and left the room.

"I'm going to go take my things back to the bunkhouse," Adam said to his mother. Without looking at her, he turned and left the house.

The next morning Maureen caught up with Adam in the barn as he was getting ready to head out into the fields. "You've been avoiding me Adam," she said.

"No..." he started to reply but stopped.

"What happened at the Shaw place?" Maureen asked.

"Nothing. We picked for a few days and then we left."

"Look at me Adam," she said. She placed her hand under his chin and lifted it until he looked her in the eye. "I've known you since before you were born. I know when something's troubling you . . . what is it?"

He looked back at her and fought back the tears. "I can't..." he said weakly.

"Adam Avery! You tell me what happened or I'll march right into the house and ask your grandmother."

He shook his head. "Don't..." he said.

"You have to. Whatever you're keeping from me is wearing on you. I'm your mother, let me help you!"

Before he knew what happened the words came tumbling out. Adam told his mother the whole story; Mr. Shaw, the housekeeper, the fire. Maureen listened with increasing shock and revulsion until he finished. She was speechless for a moment after, her face a mixture of emotions. Finally she said, "Alright, I understand why you're frightened. We'll keep this between us until I figure out what to do."

Adam wiped his eyes and nodded. He gathered up his rake and other tools and walked with his mother to the barn door. As they walked out into the daylight they found Connie standing just outside. "Oh, there you two are," she said. "Is everything alright?"

"Oh, we're fine," Maureen said cheerfully. "Ready to start the day."

Adam looked at his Aunt Connie. She was smiling but there was something behind it. He wondered if she had been listening.

CHAPTER 18

The condition of the crop had worsened while they had been away. The corn stalks were stunted and there were signs of blight on the ears. After a long day in the fields the family returned to the house for another solemn dinner. As they were clearing the table there was a loud knock on the door. "Now what?" Iris said. She looked at Connie and said, "See who it is and get rid of them.

Adam felt an overpowering urge to get out of the house so he slipped out of the dining room behind his aunt Connie and stood behind her as she answered the door. Standing there with his thumbs hitched in his belt was Deputy Silas Ferguson.

"Evening Connie," Ferguson drawled.

"Hello Silas," Connie replied cooly.

"Wondering if I could have a word with your mother?"

"About what?"

Ferguson's mouth tightened into a smirk. "I'd think it would be best if you just let me talk to her."

Connie folded her arms across her chest and started to say, "Anything you have to say to..."

"What is it?" Iris interrupted. Adam had not heard

her enter the room. When he turned around he saw that Billie and his mother had come in too.

Ferguson removed his hat and brushed past Connie into the parlor. "Evening, Mrs. Avery," he said. "Wondering if we could have a word?"

Iris narrowed her eyes. "Is this about the cows? They're all gone. Do you want to see the bones? They're in a field at the back of the property."

"No ma'am," Ferguson shook his head. He looked around the room. When he got to Adam a chill ran down Adam's spine and he looked away. "Where's Willie and your son-in-law?" he asked, turning back to Iris.

"They're in the kitchen," Iris answered peevishly. "Just say what you've come to say and be done with it!"

Ferguson smirked again and brushed something off of his hat. He looked back at Iris and said, "Seems there was a bit of trouble up at a farm near Axeville."

"What kind of trouble?" Iris said. Her face was unreadable. Adam looked over Iris' shoulder and saw Maureen turn a little pale.

"The worst kind," Ferguson said. "Man by the name of Shaw, his wife and housekeeper burned in their home."

Iris shook her head. "I don't see what that's got to do with us."

"Oh, and their foreman, some German guy. They found him in an irrigation ditch, gutted like a deer."

Iris seemed to freeze. Maureen raised her hand to her

mouth and quietly stepped back out of the room. Ferguson went on, "There was a colored family there doing some picking. They said that another family had been there and disappeared after the fire."

Willie and Leon had entered the parlor from where Maureen had just left. "I still don't see what that's got to do with us." Iris said, regaining her indignation.

"Well, that's the thing," Ferguson said, his smirk disappearing. "They said it was an older woman, a married couple, a couple of kids and," his eyes settled on Willie, "a small guy who seemed a little slow but at the same time a little evil."

The room fell quiet. Adam glanced around from one family member to another. Each one seemed to be staring straight ahead, afraid to give anything away. All except Iris, that is. Her indignation grew as she pointed a finger at Ferguson. "How dare you come into our home and make these accusations!"

"They even described a black truck," Ferguson went on, gesturing towards the front yard where the truck was parked. "The colored fella said there was some writing on the side. Pity he can't read though. He couldn't tell us what it said."

Iris was apoplectic, "Get out!" she said raising her voice. "Don't you dare bother us with this nonsense and gossip!"

Ferguson just looked at Iris for a moment, then he looked at Willie and then at Adam. Once again Adam felt his skin crawl and could feel the blood rush to his head as he averted his gaze.

"Alright," Ferguson said. "The sheriff just wanted to give you a chance to cooperate."

"You heard my wife." Leon roared. "Get the hell out of my house and don't come back unless you've come to apologize. And tell your rat bastard father to do his own dirty work next time."

Ferguson nodded and once again the smirk returned to his face. "Have it your way," he said putting his hat back on. "We'll be seeing you." With that he turned and went out the front door.

No one left in the room spoke or even looked at each other. Finally Iris wiped her hands on her apron and looked at Connie and said, "Well, we better see to those dishes. Adam took that as his signal to escape the house. He went out the front door and as he descended the steps he saw two shapes standing by Ferguson's car in the gathering darkness. He knew one was Deputy Ferguson and he was pretty sure the other one was his mother.

Adam returned to the bunk house and laid in his bed. The gas lamp was turned down low and he looked across the room at Willie's empty bed. His mind was racing with thoughts of his mother confiding a terrible secret to the man who had murdered his father. He knew she was doing what she thought was the right thing but he was terrified of what it might cost. He closed his eyes and tried to sleep, hoping when he woke up it would have turned out to all be a bad dream. He opened his eyes and looked at the ceiling and then at the crate next to his cot that served as a nightstand. The two dog eared Mark Twain novels were there. He wished he had the courage to run away like Huck Finn had, but the thought of leaving his mother behind was daunting. After a while fatigue took over and he drifted off into a fitful sleep.

He opened his eyes at daybreak to find his grandmother standing over his bed. He blinked the sleep out of his eyes and sat up. Iris had never set foot in the bunk house as far as he could remember. He looked across the room at Willie's bed and saw it was still empty.

"Adam, I have something to tell you," Iris said quietly.

"What is it?"

"Your mother is gone."

"Gone?" Adam asked. "What... gone where?"

"I don't know," Iris said shaking her head. "After deputy Ferguson left she was nowhere to be found."

Adam was dumbstruck. His eyes lost focus. Had his mother left him alone with his father's unstable family? Or had Ferguson done something to his unsuspecting mother?

"We've already called the Sheriff and asked if he knew anything but he wouldn't tell us if he did," Iris said.

Adam couldn't hold back the tears. "No," he said, his body starting to shake.

"I'm sorry dear," Iris said trying to sound comforting.

"No, no, no," Adam practically howled. "Not again."

Iris glared down at him. "Again? What do you mean, 'again?'"

Adam gritted his teeth and said, "Silas Ferguson murdered my father."

CHAPTER 19

Iris didn't seem to comprehend what Adam had told her at first. She stood looking puzzled for a moment and then asked him what he meant. Adam felt the words come spilling out about what he saw and heard the night his father died; the gunshots, Ferguson setting the shed on fire and then leaving.

"Why didn't you say something?" Iris asked.

Adam just turned away and squeezed his eyes shut. He was ashamed of how scared he had been. Scared enough to carry the burden as long as he had. Iris gave up on waiting for an answer and turned on her heel and left the bunk house.

Adam sat motionless for a while until he had the sensation that the musty walls were closing in around him. He pulled on his clothes and went outside. He couldn't bring himself to go to the house so he went to where his father had been laid to rest and stood over Jacob's grave. His mother had taught him a few prayers that he could now barely remember. The rest of the family wasn't religious at all. Iris seemed almost hostile whenever the subject was brought up. He got halfway through the Lord's Prayer and then couldn't recall the rest of it. Instead he silently asked God to look after his mother, wherever she was. He suddenly felt the urge to get as far away from the house and the family as he could. He turned to leave the grave site and saw his Aunt Connie standing at the edge of the burial ground, looking at him.

"I'm so sorry," Connie said. "I can't imagine what you're going through."

Adam cast his eyes down and said nothing. Connie walked up to where he was standing and put her hands on his shoulders. "I know you're troubled by the accident at the Shaw's farm..." she began. Adam felt his body tense up. "Accident?" he thought to himself. He looked up at Connie's face trying to read what she might be getting at. "I know you told your mother..." she paused and bit her lip. "And I don't blame you. If she left with Deputy Ferguson I know she thought she was doing the right thing. But you have to understand we're doing what we have to do to survive." She took a hand and brushed a single tear that ran down Adam's cheek. Connie pulled Adam close and softened her voice. "It will all work out," she said.

Adam freed himself gently and willed himself not to shed any more tears. "You have to be brave," Connie said. "We all do." She looked over his shoulder at Jacob's grave. "I know it's what your father would have wanted." Adam took a deep breath and nodded, if anything to get his aunt to leave him alone.

"And I hate to have to tell you this but we have to leave for a few days," Connie added.

Jacob looked at her quizzically. "What? Where?" he asked.

"Another farm," Connie replied. "A place up near Zoar Valley that the Jordans told us about."

"I can't," Jacob said. "I have to wait for my mother."

Connie smiled slightly and said, "It's just for a few days."

"Can't I stay and help Grandpa?"

"No, John needs to stay. Someone is going to need to run the tractor while we're gone."

Adam felt his grief giving way to frustration. "I don't want to go," he said quietly.

Connie put a hand on his cheek again. "I understand," she said. "But we need you and I'm afraid your Grandmother will insist." With that she turned and left him alone again in the shadow of his father's grave.

An hour later the truck was packed and they were on their way north to Zoar Valley. With John staying behind to look after Leon and the farm, Willie was pressed into driving. He was already seated behind the wheel when Adam joined Connie and Billie in the back. The truck lurched and bucked as Willie struggled with the gears and the clutch. Adam stole a glance at Billie, she was unusually withdrawn and looked like she had been crying. Connie was making a good show of it, chatting away over the sound of the truck's engine and the road.

"The Jordan's won't be there," she said. "They claim the

people who own the farm were cursed. Can you imagine? In this day and age letting some silly superstition stop you from doing an honest day's work." She shook her head. "I suppose you'll get that with 'those' people."

She prattled on about how they were going to pick an early crop of potatoes and she was sure that no one could be as cheap and dishonest as Ezra Shaw. Adam looked at his cousin Billie and tried to catch her eye. It seemed that her mother's words had upset her even further. She turned her head so she was looking away from Adam and Connie. Connie must have taken notice of Billie's reaction and she fell silent.

After a few hours the truck slowed and pulled off to the side of the road. After a moment Iris climbed out of the passenger side and looked up and down the road.

"What's wrong?" Connie asked.

Iris looked irritated. "The directions the colored man gave us," Iris said shaking her head. "The man was illiterate and barely knew any road names. I think we may have missed a turn."

"What are we going to do?" Connie asked.

"I don't know!" Iris snapped.

Just then a sedan that was heading in the other direction slowed to a stop. A middle aged man in a dirty work shirt was behind the wheel. Iris stepped around to the driver's side.

The man looked at them, stopping when he got to Willie and hesitating a moment before looking back to Iris. "Do you folks need help?" He asked.

"We're looking for the Spencer place," Iris said. "Do you know it?"

The man frowned and asked, "What do you want with them?"

If Iris was put off by the man's reaction she didn't show it. "We're pickers going to help them with their harvest," she replied.

The man seemed to consider this for a moment and then gesture with his thumb back in the direction from where he had come. "Keep on heading that way for about a mile and then turn left on Forty Road. Follow that for another mile or so and there'll be a driveway on your left. That's the Spencer farm."

"Thank you so much," Iris answered cordially.

The man nodded, gave Willie one more odd glance then put the car into gear and drove off.

They almost passed the driveway on Forty Road. It was nearly obscured by trees on either side and only marked by an old dilapidated mailbox that looked like it had been knocked off its post more that once. Adam felt a strange sense of foreboding as the truck made its way up the rutted drive. It was dark and felt closed in. The smell of dampness and manure filled the air. The truck came to a halt and Adam looked through the cab at an old one story house that looked like it was uninhabited. If it had once been painted, the paint had long since faded or peeled off. The gray wood walls almost blended in with the surrounding trees. The curtains were drawn in the windows on either side of the front door which stood closed.

Willie had turned the engine off and now the only sound was the ticking of the cooling engine. Through the truck's back window Adam saw Iris say something to Willie. Willie looked at his mother and then opened his door. He took a few hesitant steps towards the house and suddenly a large dog came racing around from the left side of the house, a low growl emitting from its chest. Willie barely had time to jump back into the truck before the animal threw its front paws on the door and began barking and growling in earnest. Adam, Connie and Billie huddled as close as possible to one another in the center of the truck bed in fright. The dog seemed to be focused on Willie, its large brown muzzle and snapping teeth inches away from the driver's side window.

"Bo!" a voice called out. The dog kept barking and growling. From where he sat in the back of the truck Adam could see the top of a man's hat coming from the same direction the dog had, "Bo! Come!" the man's voice said louder this time. The dog finally relented and dropped out of sight. Adam sat up and tentatively looked over the side of the truck bed. The dog had trotted back to the side of its master. It was then that he saw what the Jordan's had referred to as a "curse" and his aunt Connie had referred to as "a deformity." The man's hands resembled claws, as if his fingers had been fused together. Adam was at first aghast and then felt pity for the man. He had seen less advantaged people on the streets of Buffalo, hunch-backs, cripples, amputees, but never anything like this. The man looked to be in his late fifties, although it was hard to tell. He was unshaven and unkempt, though it looked like his appearance was due to hard work and not sloth.

Iris was the first one to muster the courage to climb out of the truck, she stepped towards the man with her hands clasped in front of her. "Mr. Spencer?" she asked.

"Yes," the man replied studying her. One of his hands dropped down to stroke the dog's head.

"We were told you were in need of pickers."

Spencer looked at Iris incredulously. "Is that so? And who told you that?" he asked.

"A family we worked with before, the Jordans?"

Spencer thought for a moment and then said, "Colored man and his wife and children?"

"That's them."

"Nice people, good workers. They haven't been here in a few years." Spencer held up his hand. "I had a feeling the kids were a little put off."

"I had that feeling too," Iris said nodding.

"And this wouldn't bother you or your young ones?"

"Oh no sir, they were raised to believe we're all God's children," Iris said.

"Yes," Spencer said, "So I've been told."

"So," Iris hesitated. "Do you have work for us?"

Spencer's eyes went from Iris to Willie and then towards the back of the truck. When he looked at Billie and Adam he smiled. "Matter of fact we do. One of the fields is ready to harvest. Be about two or three days work. The pay is two dollars a day with a bonus if you finish early and another if the field is cleared out completely."

"That sounds more than fair," she said.

"Have you ever picked potatoes?" Spencer asked.

"I'm afraid not sir, mostly corn and some fruit."

Spencer smiled again. "Well that shouldn't be a problem. All you need is a sturdy back and a good work ethic."

Iris raised her clasped hands in front of her chest as if she were about to pray. "I can't thank you enough Mr. Spencer. And you won't find a harder working family."

Spencer shot Iris an odd look. "We'll see," he said. "In the meantime there's a shed out back. It will be a little tight with five of you but it's clean and dry and there is a water pump behind the house. Go ahead and make yourselves at home and I'll check in on you later."

CHAPTER 20

When they reached the shed Adam climbed off the back of the truck with his father's old duffel bag and his bedroll. Willie had gotten out of the driver's side and Adam saw that Willie had a scratch on his left cheek and a black eye. Willie quickly turned away and went to the shed. Adam wondered if Willie had taken another beating from Deputy Ferguson the night before? Or had Leon done it? Adam had wondered about the scars on Willie's back and the almost fearful deference Willie paid to the old man. He thought about the previous night and his mother. Had she really left him behind? Had she gone with Ferguson to get help? His head ached and he felt nauseous again.

Spencer had been right, the shed was small, but it was clean and dry. Willie dropped his things and left immediately. Iris and Connie quietly set about organizing their things. Adam looked at Billie who stood motionless until she noticed Adam looking at her. She dropped her bag and also left the shed. Adam waited a second and then went out after her. She was walking quickly away in the opposite direction from the house. Adam jogged after her and caught up with her as she neared an opening in the tree-line.

"Billie," he called.

She stopped but didn't turn around. He walked up to her and stood next to her looking at her profile. She was pale and her eyes were red rimmed.

"What happened to my mother?" Adam asked.

She finally looked at him and said, "I don't know."

"Billie, I need you to tell me." Adam said pleading.

"I swear to God I don't know. She didn't come to our room last night and when I asked Grandma about it this morning she said your mother left with Ferguson."

Adam shook his head, "I don't believe it. Why would she leave with him?"

A tear rolled down Billie's cheek. "I asked my Ma the same thing and..." she choked off her words.

"And what?"

Billie sniffed and bit her lip. Then she said, "I can't..." Adam grabbed Billie by the arms. "What did she say?"

"She said your Mother left with Ferguson and she won't be back. She said she always hated Iris and Leon and the farm and..."

"And what?"

"...she didn't want to take you with her."

Adam shook his head again. "That's a lie!" he yelled.

Billie started shaking. "That's what I said," she said. "She slapped me hard and told me to watch my mouth or there'll be worse."

Adam looked at his cousin and felt his anger turn to sympathy. He recognized that Billie was in the same situation he was, living in fear and doubt about the future. He put his arms around her and she rested her head on his shoulder. They stood like that for a while and then broke off their embrace. Billie wiped the tears from her eyes and said, "We should be getting back."

As they approached the shed they saw Spencer making his way from the house with another man. Spencer was carrying a basket and seemed to be walking at a slower pace to accommodate the man he was with. Adam was relieved that the dog was nowhere in sight. As they got closer Adam saw that the man had the same disfigured, claw like hands. He looked older than Spencer and was gaunt and pale.

Spencer saw Adam and Billie and said, "There's two of 'em Jesse." The other man looked at them and smiled. "Hello," he said.

"Sorry I didn't catch your names," Spencer said.

"I'm Adam and this is my cousin Billie Jean."

Spencer held out the basket. "I'm Tom," he said. "And this is my brother, Jesse." It's just the two of us and we usually don't make much of a fuss about supper, but we managed to fix some sandwiches."

Adam took the basket and said, "Thank you."

"Jesse and I turn in early and we like to get started early," Tom said.

"Yes sir," Adam replied, understanding Tom's meaning.

"We'll be up before sun-up."

"That's a good lad," Jesse said with a wheeze in his voice. "We'll see you in the morning. Regards to the rest of your family." He tipped his hat and the two brothers turned to go back to the house.

The family ate in relative silence. Once they finished Willie disappeared again. They took turns washing at the pump and then returned to the shed. Iris took out her sewing kit and she and Connie busied themselves darning socks. Adam sat outside reading until it started to get dark. When he went inside Billie was already in bed, facing the wall. Iris and Connie were getting ready to turn in also.

"You had better get some sleep," Iris said to Adam without looking at him.

"Yes ma'am," Adam replied.

He lay awake until he heard Willie return and creep over to his bed in the corner. His mind was racing, he knew in his heart that his mother would never voluntarily leave him. What had really happened last night? He had no idea how long he lay there but after a while he could feel the walls of the shed closing in on him. He listened to his family breathing and snoring and when he was convinced they were all asleep, quietly pulled on his shirt and shoes and crept out of the shed. The night air had cooled and felt good on his face. It felt like he could breathe again. A sliver of moonlight gave the area around the shed a pale blue light. Wanting to get away from the shed without getting lost he followed the gravel path towards the house.

He heard the low growl and he froze. From out of the shadows Spencer's dog approached him slowly. His father had told him back in Buffalo that if one of the stray mongrels on the city streets approaches you should only run as a last resort. The dog came closer, his short brown coat gray in the moonlight. Adam fought the urge to turn tail and run with all his will. The dog was right in front of him now. He growled again but this time it had seemed to lose some of its menace. Adam almost flinched when it raised its great head up to his hand and sniffed at it. Then he noticed the dog's tail come up and begin to wag.

"Don't worry about old Bo, son." Adam looked up for the voice and saw Tom Spencer emerge from the same shadow the dog had. "He only acts ornery when he thinks there's a threat."

Spencer was smoking a pipe and had a shotgun cradled in his arm. "He does enjoy a good scratch behind the ears though," he added.

Slowly, Adam reached his hand to the back of Bo's head and gently scratched it. Bo immediately sat down and placed a large paw on Adam's foot. Adam looked down at the dog. In the pale light he could see that part of his right ear was missing and there was a scratch on one of his large soulful eyes.

"How long have you had him?" Adam asked.

"'Bout five years or so," Tom Spencer replied. "My brother and I were in Warsaw picking up some supplies and there was a man about to put him down. Seems like he had lost a fight and his owner didn't have any use for him. Told the man we'd give him five dollars for him and he handed him over."

Adam looked down at Bo again and wondered how anyone could be so callous with a creature's life, "Can't you sleep son?" Spencer's voice brought him back to the present. "Too stuffy in the shed?"

"No sir... the shed's fine."

Spencer puffed on his pipe and considered Adam. "Something troubling you?" he asked.

Adam felt his face flush and hoped Spencer didn't notice in the pale light. "Just restless I guess," he replied.

"I know what that's like." Spencer said sympathetically. "We've had some of the local boys come out with vandalism on their minds so once in a while Bo will hear something and we'll come out and have a walk around."

Adam considered that and wondered if the boys that Spencer was referring to had singled out the Spencer brothers because they were different. Spencer seemed to be reading his mind. "You get used to it," he said gesturing with the hand holding the pipe. "My brother and I have put up with people staring and whispering all of our lives." He smiled and shook his head. "Some people even think it was witchcraft that did this to us."

"You were born that way?" Adam heard himself ask. He hadn't meant to be rude but his curiosity had gotten the better of him.

If Spencer was put off, he didn't show it. "Yep," he said. "Matter of fact there used to be quite a few of us all through the valley. At first there were all kinds of theories about it; a virus, a curse, even the Devil himself. But then a few years back a couple of doctors traced us all back to an English woman who had settled here in the eighteen hundreds." He shook his head. "Turns out it she had a sickness that was prevalent in her profession and it caused most of her male descendants to be born this way."

"You said there were more people like you and your brother in the valley?" Adam asked

"There were," Spencer replied somberly. "We're dying out. About ten years ago most of us came to an agreement that we would never get married or have children of our own. We didn't want to curse another generation."

Adam felt pity for Spencer and his brother, but also admired the selflessness that they showed by choosing a life of loneliness as opposed to risking passing their condition on to an innocent child as they once had been. He couldn't fathom what it had been like to grow up in a world that thought you were a freak or spawn of the Devil. But then the thought of Spencer only having his sickly brother as family reminded him of his own situation and the pain came back. He looked down at his feet and fought back a fresh wave of tears.

"You sure you're alright?" Spencer asked.

"Yes sir," Adam said, trying to sound as composed as possible. "I should be getting back."

"Well, goodnight then Adam."

"Goodnight Mr. Spencer," Adam turned and walked back to the shed.

CHAPTER 21

The next morning Adam was the first one up, awoken by a dream about his parents, the details of which he couldn't immediately recall, only that they were trying to tell him something and he couldn't understand them. He lay on his bedroll damp with sweat for a while and then a cock crowed in the distance. The sun rose somewhere behind a steel gray cloud cover, it looked like the drought might be nearing an end. It was already muggy and the air seemed stagnant.

After a modest breakfast of bread and coffee the family met the Spencer brothers at the barn. Bo was there and seemed to be eyeing Willie up like he was waiting for Willie to do something. Tom Spencer started up an old tractor that looked like it was long past its prime and had the family climb on the trailer for the ride out to the fields. His brother walked slowly behind with Bo keeping pace. Adam noticed that Jesse Spencer didn't look any healthier than he had the day before; his skin was gray and slack on his face. He smiled easily but Adam wondered how able he was to help his brother run the farm.

They arrived at the end of a field and Tom Spencer gave each member of the party a small pitch fork and a burlap bag. There was a quick tutorial on how to ease the potatoes out of the loose, sandy dirt and then they were each assigned a row and went to work.

The humid air made Adam perspire as he diligently worked his way down the row. It was still better than picking corn he thought. He looked over and saw Tom Spencer working alongside Billie. He thought about Ezra Shaw and how he seemed to look down at the people working for him. Spencer, in contrast was digging in the dirt with them.

Adam lost track of time but before he knew it he was at the end of his row. He looked back and saw that Willie wasn't far behind. Iris and Billie were farther back and Connie was slightly behind them, the weight of her bag slowing her down.

"See? Nothing to it" Tom said, mopping his brow with a handkerchief.

"Shall I start another row?" Adam asked.

Spencer withdrew a pocket watch from his overalls and looked at it. "No, we'll take a break and let the women folk catch their breath." He looked up and smiled at Adam. "But I do appreciate your work ethic young man."

"Thomas," Jesse Spencer's voice interrupted them as he approached with Bo in tow. He had a concerned look on his face. "I was just over at the South field and the Aphids are back.

"Dang it!" Tom Spencer said. "I was hoping we wouldn't have to spray again."

Adam knew about Aphids, a small green insect that would eat the leaves off a healthy plant. The farm back home had been plagued with them one summer.

"We'll have to," Jesse said. "The field's thick with them."

Willie had finished his row and walked up to where they were standing. Tom Spencer looked at Adam and Willie. "Alright," he said. "Looks like you folks have the hang of this. There's a water can in the trailer, take a break and then start a new row. I'm going to get the arsenic out of the barn and spray the other field."

"Yes sir," Adam said.

"And tell your family to steer clear of where I'll be spraying. That stuff is bad for you even if you breath in a little of it."

After another row they broke for lunch and then two more rows and it was quitting time. Iris had left early to start dinner and there was soup and bread waiting when they got back to the shed. The heat had curbed Adam's appetite but he knew he should eat to keep his strength up. After they finished their meal, they cleaned up. Billie caught Adam's eye and motioned for him to follow her. They were walking away from the shed when Connie called out to them. "Where are you two going?"

"Just down by the creek Ma," Billie answered.

Connie frowned and looked at them. "Well, be careful. And don't be gone too long."

They followed a path that cut down to Cattaraugus Creek as it made a slow bend that formed a natural boundary around the Spencer farm. Billie had noticed it on the way back from the field. She took off her shoes and stepped in. The water was shallow but clear and Adam did the same. The water was cool on his skin and felt fantastic. He looked up and noticed Billie wading across the bend in the creek. The current must have made the water deeper on the other side because as she got past the middle it was up over her knees. Unlike the time back at the Avery farm, she didn't take off her dress, instead she leaned forward and fell face down in the water. Adam watched for a moment as she drifted towards the far bank. She didn't seem to be moving at all, just drifting. Adam waded over to where she was and looked down at her. Her long brown hair was splayed out in the water. "Billie," he said. There was no response. "Billie!" he said louder. Still no sign of movement. He reached down and put one hand on her arm and the other around her waist and gently pulled her out of the water. Her eyes were closed and she had a serene look on her face. She said nothing.

"What are you doing?" Adam asked.

She opened her eyes and looked into his. "Trying to get away, if only for a minute," she replied. Adam understood. He raised her to her feet and embraced her. Her body was cool and damp against his. He felt a stirring in his body and immediately felt ashamed. He forced it out of his mind and replaced it with the urge to protect her. He'd stood silent when his father was killed and had failed to protect his mother. He swore to himself that nothing would happen to Billie.

"They're planning something," she said quietly into his shoulder.

Adam held her at arm's length and looked into her eyes. "Iris? Willie?" he asked.

"And my mother" Billie said.

"What are they planning?"

Billie shook her head. "I don't know. They were whispering to each other this morning at the barn. When they saw me they stopped and acted like nothing was going on."

Adam's mind flashed back to the scene at Ezra Shaw's farm; Shaw laid out on the floor, his shut-in wife hiding upstairs in a burning house, and he could still hear the screaming of the housekeeper. He thought about the Spencer brothers. Hadn't they suffered enough in their lifetime?

He looked back towards the path. "I have to stop them," he heard himself say aloud.

"I know," Billie agreed. "I can't stand the thought of them hurting anyone else. But what can we do?" Adam looked back at Billie. The blank stare she'd had when he pulled her out of the water was replaced by a look of concern.

"I have an idea."

CHAPTER 22

S omething's wrong." Adam opened his eyes and found Billie leaning over him shaking his shoulder. The first hint of another overcast sunrise was making its way through the shed's window.

"What is it?" he asked sitting up.

"Willie and Ma and Grandma are gone.

Adam looked around the shed and sure enough, their bedrolls and bags were gone. He quickly pulled on his shirt and shoes and bolted from the shed. The humidity was already stifling and his shirt was soaked with sweat as he ran up the drive towards the house. The family's truck was sitting by the side of the house with the engine idling, there was no one in the cab. He rounded the corner to the front of the house and saw Willie climbing the steps with his .22 caliber rabbit gun pointed at the ground. Iris and Connie were a few feet behind him. Connie looked anxious, Iris looked determined. Adam stopped in his tracks. They all looked at him and froze.

Willie didn't have time to react as the door swung open and Tom Spencer emerged with his 12 gauge shotgun pointed at Willie's head. "Drop it son," he said calmly.

Willie seemed to consider his options. A brief look of anger and defiance crossed his face until Spencer tightened his deformed finger around the trigger. "Don't," Spencer said.

Willie flinched and then gently laid the rifle down at his feet. Spencer pushed the barrel of the shotgun into Willie's chest and Willie stepped back until he fell off the porch step and landed on the ground. Jesse Spencer emerged from the door with an ancient revolver at his side. Jesse climbed down the stairs and pointed the gun at Willie who had started to crabwalk away from the porch.

"What did you do to Bo?" Jesse growled.

"I... nothing," Willie stammered.

"He's in the house, looking like he's going to die, you son of a bitch!" Jesse yelled and then started to cough.

"Jesse!" Tom Spencer yelled. He stepped next to his brother and looked at him. "Bo will be alright."

"How dare you!" Iris exclaimed.

"You shut your mouth!" Jesse snapped at her. "You and this half-wit meant us harm. You poisoned our dog and you were going to rob us!"

"That's absurd!" Iris yelled back.

"Is it?" Tom Spencer said. "We heard what happened to old man Shaw and his wife and it didn't take long to figure out you were up to no good. Now I'm going to have to ask you to get off our land."

"You can't do this," Iris wouldn't give up. "You owe us a day's wages and you're treating us like criminals."

Tom took a hand off the shotgun and with it still leveled at Willie dug into his pocket. He pulled out a few dollars and dropped them at Willie's feet. "That should cover it."

"This will not stand!" Iris hissed. "We'll go to the law!"

The corners of Tom's mouth turned up. He took a step back and leveled the shotgun at Willie again. "You do that," he said. "I'm sure that would be an interesting conversation." He looked at Iris and added, "Just be sure your righteous indignation will only carry you so far."

"You can't speak to me like that," Iris replied. "The Jordan's were right, you are an abomination."

Billie had walked up and stood next to Adam. Tom Spencer gestured in their direction. "People have been saying that about us for years," he said. "I don't know about that but I know you should be ashamed of yourself for what you're doing to those children."

Iris looked like she was going to say something in response but instead she looked down at Willie and said, "Get up out of the dirt boy. Let's get out of this God forsaken place. Iris, Willie and Connie started to walk quickly around the side of the house and when their backs were turned to Tom Spencer he gave Adam a wink.

^^^

It started to rain on the drive back to the Hollow, the first fat drops splashing down onto the top of the truck with a loud *thwack*. Then it rained in earnest, sheets of rain coming down reducing the visibility to just a few feet. Willie was forced to pull off to the side of the road. Connie crammed herself into the cab with Iris and Willie while Billie and Adam huddled together under a tarp that had been brought along to cover their luggage.

"Did you warn Mr. Spencer? Billie raised her voice against the sound of the rain hitting the tarp.

"Yes."

"And Grandma doesn't know, does she?"

Adam shook his head. "Mr. Spencer said he'd keep it a secret." He looked down suddenly.

"What is it?" Billie asked, picking up on his discomfort.

Adam looked back at her. "He said you and me could stay with them if we wanted to. He said we shouldn't have to live like this."

Billie looked into his eyes for a moment. "I understand Adam."

"You understand what?" he looked at her quizzically.

"You want to get back to your Ma."

Adam cast his gaze downward again and he saw it against his hip. A large metal can with a skull and crossbones on it that hadn't been in the truck before they were at the Spencer farm.

^^^

After a while rain let up and they set off South again back towards Napoli and the Hollow. Connie had returned to the back of the truck with them and didn't say a word the entire trip home. Occasionally she would look at Billie with a mixture of disappointment and pity, but she wouldn't look at her daughter for long before drifting off into her thoughts. The wet, pock marked roads made the trip back to the Hollow seem interminable. Finally, around six that evening they made their way up Merchant Hill Road. As they turned into the drive Adam noticed that the family's sign was tilting away from the road and weeds had grown several feet up around the post it was mounted on. Willie pulled the truck up to the front of the house.

Everyone was tired and wet from the long slog home. Adam wearily climbed off the back of the truck and grabbed his things. He was headed to the bunkhouse when he heard Iris say, "Now what?" He looked towards the house. The screen door was hanging off of one hinge and the wooden door was open. The house was dark and quiet. Curious he followed his grandmother inside.

Leon was sitting in a chair in the parlor. His hair was a tangled mess on his head and he was wearing a filthy undershirt and trousers. The room smelled of must and human waste.

"Where is John?" Iris asked sharply.

Leon raised his head and looked at her like he hadn't heard the question. The others had entered the room. "Where is John?" Iris asked again, raising her voice.

"Gone," Leon muttered.

"Gone? Where? When did he leave?"

Again, Leon stared blankly at Iris, who was quickly

losing patience. She turned to Connie and snapped, "Open the windows. The stench in here!" Then she pointed at Willie and Adam. "Take him out to the porch and get a pail of water."

Adam swallowed and looked at his grandfather. Uncle John had left the old man to fend for himself and he'd not done well at it. He wondered what contributed the most; the home-made liquor or the stroke. He glanced at Willie who thankfully didn't look back. Instead Willie was looking at his father with a mixture of fear and revulsion.

"Now!" Iris' voice pierced the silence. Despite Leon having lost weight from being malnourished, his six foot two inch frame was still hard to move. He didn't resist but he didn't help much either. Adam had to breathe through his mouth to keep from gagging as he helped Leon out onto a rocker on the porch. As soon as they had him seated Willie bolted from the porch back towards the bunkhouse.

Thankfully Adam wasn't asked to bathe his grandfather. Connie and Iris stripped off his soiled clothes and washed him and dressed him in a clean nightshirt. A tin of pork and beans was heated up and Connie spoon fed her father with a tear in her eye. Billie had found a can of creamed corn and heated it up and she and Adam were eating in the Kitchen when Iris came in. Her face was dour and her gray eyes piercing. "Go find Willie," she said to Adam. "Bring him back here and help us put your grandfather to bed." Adam silently rose and went out through the kitchen door.

He was on his way to the bunkhouse to look for Willie

when he found him in the family cemetery kneeling by Jacob's grave. Like the rest of the family, Adam had never seen Willie pray or do anything remotely religious. He cautiously walked up to Willie and cleared his throat. Willie half turned towards Adam and wiped his face. "Grandma wants us back at the house," Adam said.

Getting Leon upstairs was no easy task. He was slightly more cognizant now and definitely smelled better but he was still weak and his left leg almost useless from the stroke. Billie had been tasked with making up his bed and had aired out the room. Adam and Willie finally got Leon in the room and sat him on the edge of the bed. They stepped away and Connie walked up to her father and put her hand on his shoulder. "Dad? Did John say where he was going?"

Leon looked at her through narrowed eyes. "Bastard," he slurred.

"Dad? Did he say he'd be back?"

"Didn't say anything... left..."

Connie grimaced and pushed gently at Leon's shoulder. "Okay Dad. Lie down now."

Leon tried to knock her hand away. Connie took a step back. "Get me a drink!" he said.

"Everyone get out." Iris had come into the room unnoticed and spoke now. She stepped aside and Willie, Adam and Connie left to go downstairs. Adam looked for Billie but didn't see her. He needed to get out of the house so he went out the front door and ran as fast and as far as he could. He had no destination in mind just to get as far away from the house and the family as he could. He ran into the field at the North end of the property between the dried, malnourished corn stalks. He developed a pain in his side and ran out of breath so he slowed to a walk. Suddenly he came to a clearing. The bleached bones and ashes from where the dairy herd had been burned were strewn forlornly around the clearing. Adam stopped and bent over, putting his hands on his knees. He couldn't breathe. He couldn't cry. It was if everything had been sucked out of him.

CHAPTER 23

The sky cleared the next day and the heat came back with it. Thankfully the humidity had dissipated somewhat but it was still blistering out in the fields. Connie, Billie and Adam had been tasked with going out into the fields and seeing if there was any corn that was worth salvaging. Willie was out hunting rabbit and squirrel and Iris was trying to restore order to her house while she tended to Leon.

The yield was dismal. They covered most of the acreage in the morning and only found a few bushels worth picking. The rest of the corn had either been affected by the drought or blight. They were returning to the house at lunchtime when Deputy Silas Ferguson pulled up in his patrol vehicle. A rage grew inside Adam. He wanted to rush Ferguson and demand to know what had become of his mother. Just then Iris emerged from the front of the house scowling and wiping her hands on her apron.

"Morning, Mrs. Avery," Ferguson said tipping his hat.

"Deputy," Iris responded.

"I came out the other day to have a talk with you folks and John said you were off picking potatoes."

"That's true," Iris said. "What did you want to talk about now?"

"Well, When I heard you were off at another farm I was hoping nothing bad happened like at the Shaw place," Ferguson said smugly.

"This again?" Iris shook her head. "Don't you have anything better to do than harass us?"

Ferguson smiled. "Well it seems that a family of migrant pickers swore they were on their way to the Shaw place and they stopped here." He stopped and waited for a reaction. Iris stared at him, stone-faced. Ferguson went on, "They claim that while they were here somebody sabotaged their vehicle."

Adam looked at his grandmother, her face gave nothing away. "And you took the word of a bunch of drifters?" she said.

Ferguson chuckled softly and looked around the yard. "Where is old Willie-boy anyway?" he asked.

"He's around here somewhere," Iris said. The two looked at each other for a moment and then Iris added, "Why don't you come inside and we'll wait for Willie. I'm sure we can straighten this all out."

Ferguson thought for a moment and then said, "Alright, We'll do that." Then he followed Iris into the house.

Adam couldn't believe it, lawman or not Ferguson was evil and now his grandmother was treating him like a guest. He followed Ferguson at a distance. When they reached the parlor Iris looked at Billie and said, "Billie Jean, be a dear and go get your uncle Willie. He's probably down by the creek checking his traps."

"Yes Ma'am," Billie said and then she was gone.

The group moved into the kitchen where Ferguson took a seat at the table. Iris removed her apron and looked at him. "Silas, I'm sure we'll figure out this whole thing has been a misunderstanding."

Ferguson looked back at her with mirth in his eyes. "Is that so?"

The sarcasm didn't seem to register with Iris. "Our families have know each other for a long time, even done business together."

"That is true," Ferguson nodded.

"We don't want any trouble..." she paused.

"No, of course not."

"Well maybe we can come to some kind of understanding," she added with hope in her voice.

Ferguson looked at her quizzically. "Go on?"

"A new business arrangement."

He shook his head. "Still too much heat to go back into moonshine."

Adam felt the hair on the back of his neck stand up.

"No," Iris laughed. "Something else. But speaking of which, I still have a bottle of Leon's private stock upstairs. Would you care for a taste?"

Ferguson looked at her warily. "It's a little early," he said.

"It's John's good stuff."

"Well, a taste won't hurt I guess." Ferguson said.

Connie spoke up from the corner, "I'll get it mother."

Iris looked at her quickly. "No dear, I need to check on your father anyway. Why don't you go to the pantry and get the good glasses for us?"

Connie turned to leave and Iris looked at Adam. "Adam, would you go get some fresh water for us." Ferguson looked at Adam as if for the first time. Their eyes met and Adam's blood went cold. He finally looked away and went out to the pump.

When he came back Iris was seated at the table with Ferguson. "We didn't mean it to happen that way but things got out of hand and well..."

Ferguson looked at her seriously but said nothing. "Well, we took the money and there's no going back," Iris went on. "I know, come judgement day, I'll have to answer for what we've done, but you have to understand, the man was out to cheat us and we're struggling to get by as it is."

Ferguson thought for a moment. "How much money was in the box?" he asked.

"Over two hundred dollars," Iris replied.

Ferguson scratched his chin. "That is interesting . . . I'll tell you what. I'll take half of that and whatever you made on your last little trip up to Zoar Valley and we'll consider this investigation closed."

Anger flashed in Iris' eyes but then quickly disappeared. "Silas..." she hesitated and looked away. "I suppose this isn't a negotiation?" she added.

Ferguson chuckled. "No ma'am, it's not. But don't consider it unreasonable. The whole thing gets swept under the rug as long as we have an understanding."

"What would that be?" Iris asked.

"I understand you're doing what you have to do to get along in these hard times. Just remember who's looking out for you if you should happen to have any more of these... adventures."

Iris thought for a moment and then a slight smile crossed her face. "I guess that's fair," she said. She stood up and walked over and opened up a cabinet and removed the strong box that had been taken from the Shaws. She put it up on the counter. Then she walked back over to the table and poured a healthy measure of whiskey into a glass and offered it to Ferguson. "Well, should we have a toast to our new arrangement?"

Ferguson looked at the glass. "Where's yours?" he asked.

"Oh, I'm not much for the whiskey. I had a Tom Collins once in Jamestown and I thought I was going to die."

Ferguson smiled. "Well I guess old Leon drank enough for the two of you," he said smugly.

Adam wanted to scream. Was his grandmother really making a pact with the Devil himself. Ferguson took a deep drink and wiped his mouth. He held the glass out and looked at it. "This tastes a little off," he said.

"It shouldn't," Iris smiled. "Leon said it was John's best batch."

Ferguson shrugged and downed the rest of the glass. "Another before you go?" Iris asked offering the bottle.

"Nope," Ferguson said rising. "I've got to head over to the Lawson's. They claim somebody's been in their hen house." A bead of sweat ran down his forehead. He blinked his eyes and then looked at Iris.

"Something wrong, deputy?" she asked.

He stared at her for a moment and then doubled over clutching his stomach.

"Are you unwell?" she asked.

Ferguson put his hand on the table and then collapsed back into the chair. "What..." he started. Suddenly Willie rushed in from outside through the backdoor with his knife out and ready. Iris held out her hand to stop him and he obliged. Ferguson looked from Willie to Iris and said, "You bitch!" He gagged and then fell to the floor in a fetal position. His breathing became labored and then he vomited. He tried to crawl but his body started to convulse.

"Oh my God!" Connie cried from the doorway where she was standing with Billie.

Adam stepped over to where Ferguson was and leaned over him. He grabbed the front of Ferguson's shirt and rolled him on his back.

"Adam!" Iris yelled.

Vomit was covering Ferguson's chin and blood was coming from his nose. Adam knew he was dying. "Where is my mother?" he screamed. Ferguson made gurgling noises so

Adam looked into the deputy's eyes for an answer. All he saw
was terror and confusion and then the light went out from Silas
Ferguson's eyes. Adam released his grip and stood up looking
down at Ferguson. Here was the cause of so much misery lying
dead at his feet and he felt nothing except the empty realization
that he may never know what had happened to his mother.

"Oh my God," Connie repeated, quieter this time. She
looked at Iris and asked, "What have you done?"

"Get a hold of yourself," Iris snapped. "I did what I had
to do. There was no money to give him remember? Your no ac-
count husband made off with it when he deserted you and your
daughter."

Connie grimaced and started to cry. "What are we
going to do? They'll come looking for him," she said pointing
at the body on the floor.

Iris looked at Willie who was staring at the body,
breathing heavily. "Willie!" she snapped. Take Adam out to the
graveyard and start digging a grave."

Willie looked at his mother confused. Connie let out a
sob and said, "You're just going to bury him in the family plot?"

Iris glared at Connie and then her features softened
slightly. "I didn't have a chance to tell you all..." she hesitated.

"Tell us what?" Billie asked.

"Your father passed this morning," Iris said flatly. She
pointed at Ferguson's body. "We're going to bury him underneath Leon."

The kitchen fell silent. Adam looked at the bottle on

the table that Iris had retrieved from Leon's bedside. No one moved or even seemed to breathe for a moment until Iris spoke. "Can you drive the deputy's car?" she asked looking at Billie.

"I think so," Billie replied.

"Then take it to the back of the fields where the cows are and come back." Iris turned to Connie. "Clean this mess up after they move the deputy."

No one moved until Iris yelled, "Now!"

It took Willie and Adam all afternoon and early evening to dig a hole in the dry, hardened ground big enough for two bodies. Neither one spoke as they toiled, they just worked at the dirt with picks and shovels. At dusk they rolled Ferguson's body into the grave and then went up to retrieve Leon. At least Iris or Connie had wrapped him in a sheet for his burial. They labored to bring him downstairs and through the kitchen and out to the cemetery. When he was finally in the grave they stood for a moment and caught their breath. Willie picked up a shovel then and started to throw dirt into the grave. Adam picked up a shovel and started doing the same. Adam glanced at Willie and in the fading light he could see tears welling in his uncle's eyes. Willie was speaking between shovels full of dirt as he worked. It was barely audible to Adam. "Never... hit me... again..." was all Adam could make out.

They finished just after dark and walked towards the house. Iris was waiting for them at the back door. "You boys wash up and turn in. We'll be heading out early in the morning."

"Where we goin' Ma?" Willie asked wearily.

"The one place I thought I'd never go back to," Iris said. "We're going to see my family in Conewango." She closed the door and turned out the porch light.

CHAPTER 24

Despite Adam's curiosity he couldn't bring himself to ask Willie what Iris meant by "her family." His father had never mentioned his maternal grandparents at all when he was alive. Willie was still acting oddly after the day's events so Adam let it rest.

Up at dawn the next morning and the family set off for Conewanga Valley on the western edge of Cattaraugus County. The sun was shining brightly again but the breeze in the back of the truck made it bearable. Past farmland and forests and a terrain that grew hillier every mile, the truck struggling up the inclines. After a few hours they were on Route 62 headed north when Willie pulled off the road while Iris consulted a map.

"Where are we going?" Billie whispered to Connie.

"Your grandmother's family has a farm near here." Connie replied softly.

"She never talked about her family before." Billie said.

Connie held a finger up to her lips and peered into the cab to see if Iris was listening. When she was satisfied that Iris was giving Willie directions she whispered, "She had a falling out with her father." With that Connie looked off, effectively ending the conversation. A short while later Willie turned the truck off on a rutted dirt track and bumped along for about fifty yards until they came up to a small house. Adam stood up and looked at the house. It was small and in a state of disrepair. The roof was sagging in the middle and the front porch looked like it was about to collapse. Iris climbed out of the passenger seat and stood looking towards the house.

"It looks deserted," Billie whispered to Adam.

Connie must've heard her because she interjected, "They're probably out in the fields dear."

There was a buggy off to the side with rusty wheels and it's paint flaking. A white horse emerged from around the far side of the house and looked at them curiously. It's hair was mottled and dirty and it's ribs were showing. Iris walked up to the front of the house and carefully climbed the step onto the porch. She hesitated for a moment and then knocked on the door. After a moment the door opened and a man looked out at Iris. He was in his fifties with a white beard and he was wearing a white shirt and black pants. Adam had seen Amish people in Buffalo when he was younger. His mother had explained their odd customs and disdain for modern conveniences. He found it hard to fathom that his grandmother Iris, one of the most anti-religious people he had ever met was once a member of the Amish community. The family had climbed off the truck and the man looked at them all one at a time and then back at Iris with a look of confusion. Finally he said, "Yes?"

"Isaac?" Iris said.

The man looked more confused. "It's me, Sarah," Iris added.

Isaac's expression changed from confusion to surprise to anger. "Sarah? He asked.

"Yes."

Isaac shook his head. "I'm sure you haven't forgotten Father sent you away."

"No I haven't." Iris said sharply. "Nor have I forgiven him for what he did."

"You always were headstrong. Never willing to atone."

"I was willing to atone," Iris replied. "I was sorry for what I did to mother but I'm not sorry for not bending to what father tried to pass off as 'God's will.'"

Isaac frowned. "Abram Schrock was a good man, a pious man. He would have made a good husband."

"Abram Schrock was a monster!" Iris exclaimed. "He put his first wife in the ground and then father bartered me off to him like I was livestock."

"I'll not stand here and let you speak poorly of my father and blaspheme the Lord!" Isaac shouted. "Go back to your English and your heathen ways.

They stood and stared at each other for a moment. A small boy, about five years of age peered out from around Isaac. Iris looked at the boy and then back at Isaac. She gestured over her shoulder and said, "This is my family Isaac. We need help."

"You gave up the right to come here with your hand out when you got yourself excommunicated." Isaac said and started to close the door.

"Isaac! I am your sister, your family." Iris implored. "What would the bible say about turning us away in our time of need?"

Isaac paused for a moment and then said, "There is nothing here for you Sarah."

"What kind of example are you setting for your boy there?" She asked pointing at the boy who had shrunk behind Isaac's legs.

"My grandson?" Isaac said looking back at the boy. "Samuel is deaf. He hasn't heard a word we've said."

"Where are his parents?" Iris asked.

"My daughter died in childbirth," he replied grimly. Her husband went out to find work as a carpenter and I haven't seen him in a year."

"And your wife?" Iris asked.

Isaac peered out at Iris. "Smallpox. Ruth passed twenty years ago. It's just me and the boy now."

"What about the neighbors?"

"Gone. They left in '29."

Iris shook her head. "They told father not to come back here," she said quietly. "We should have never left Lancaster."

"He was born here!" Isaac said. "This land belonged to his family."

"And they left here and went back home. You were too young to remember but the only reason father wanted to leave Lancaster was he couldn't get along with the elders."

"Whatever his reason was he was your father! You are commanded by the Lord to honor him."

Iris stepped back and folded her arms across her chest. "I'm sorry brother. I know I disappointed you and mother but I did what I thought I had to."

Isaac seemed to consider that. He continued to stare at her. "We've been on the road all day. I know you're a righteous man and I don't want to put you out any further."

Isaac waited. Iris clasped her hands in front of her. "All I ask is that you let us stay here tonight and then in the morning we'll go and you'll never see us again."

Now Isaac crossed his arms. He looked past Iris at Billie and Adam. "Alright," he said. "For the sake of the children. It is the Christian thing to do. You may take shelter in the barn for the night."

Iris bowed her head, "Thank you brother," she said.

No one dared ask Iris about what had just been discussed. Judging by the look on Connie's face Adam surmised that no one, with the possible exception of Leon, knew of Iris's background. He wondered if Leon had met her when she was still calling herself Sarah.

The family retired to a small barn behind the house. It was empty inside except for some rusted farm implements and a plow with a broken harness on it. Willie built a fire and Iris heated up a tin of beans and served it with a loaf of stale bread she had brought from the Hollow. The family ate in relative silence and then took their dishes to the pump behind the house to wash. Afterwards Iris walked off towards the back of the property without saying a word. Willie and Connie returned dejectedly to the barn, leaving Billie and Adam by themselves.

"I can't believe it," Billie said as they started to walk slowly in the opposite direction that Iris had gone..

"It might explain why she is the way she is," Adam replied.

"What do you mean?"

"Why she isn't a church person. Why she's so angry all the time."

Billie looked down and thought. "I suppose that could be," she said.

Adam continued, "I'm ashamed to say I have my own doubts."

"Doubts about what?"

Adam felt himself choking up. "My mother always talked about how God would look after us."

Billie looked at him. "Neither of my parents are very religious," she offered. She put a hand on his cheek. "One thing my father always said was 'Heaven helps he who helps himself.' I thought that he just used that as an excuse to do whatever he wanted but maybe it's true."

They both looked up. Isaac's grandson Samuel was standing in front of them. His hair was light blond and his blue eyes were looking at them with curiosity. Billie took a step towards Samuel and the boy half turned and looked like he was ready to bolt back to the house. Billie stopped and smiled at

Samuel. He looked at Billie and turned back to face her full on.

"He's deaf you know," Adam said.

Billie glanced over at Adam and said, "I know. And he's probably not seen too many people like us before. You could try smiling."

Adam didn't feel like smiling but he did so to humor his cousin. Samuel was about fifteen feet away and Billie stepped forward to close the distance. Samuel looked nervously over his shoulder and then back at Billie. Billie widened her smile and crouched down so she was eye level with him. "What have you got in your hand?" She asked pointing to it.

"He can't hear you?" Adam whispered impatiently.

"Maybe he can read lips," she responded.

Samuel tentatively walked forward a few steps and held up his hand. He had a small wooden horse.

"A horse?" Billie gasped enthusiastically. A slight smile came across Samuel's face. Billie sat down on the ground and then Samuel closed the rest of the distance between them. He held out the horse to show Billie. "You see?" Billie glanced back at Adam. "He may not be able to hear but he understands."

Suddenly Isaac rushed up from the house. "What are you doing?" He yelled. His face was flushed with anger. Adam stepped forward and stood next to Billie.

Billie looked up and said, "He was showing us his horse."

Samuel whirled around when he saw Billie look up but it was too late, Isaac cuffed him in the ear and grabbed him by the shirt collar. "Stay away from him!" Isaac growled. He turned and dragged the boy back towards the house. Billie stood up and started after them but Adam put his hand on her arm. Billie glared at him and a tear rolled down her cheek.

"What..." Adam started.

"What kind of life does that little boy have to look forward to?" Billie asked.

"What do you mean?"

"No parents? No schooling? Just this run down farm and that angry old man."

Adam shook his head. "I agree, but what else could he hope for."

"Have you ever heard of Helen Keller?"

"I think so," Adam answered uncertainly.

"She's deaf and blind but she learned sign language and went to college and now she writes books and gives lectures. Samuel is a human being and that old man treats him like he's some kind of animal."

Adam fell silent. He felt sorry for the boy but what could they do? "We should get back," he said.

Billie stood for a moment looking towards where Isaac and Samuel had gone and then she wiped her face, turned around and walked back towards the barn.

CHAPTER 25

As the first light of day crept through the trees the family was up and moving, loading the truck for the trip back to the Hollow. When they were loaded and making their way past the house the truck slowed and then came to a halt by the back door. Iris climbed out of the passenger seat and Willie turned the engine off.

Adam's mind was racing, what was Iris up to? She wouldn't steal from her own family would she? Willie climbed out of the driver's side and gave Adam a dirty look. This time Adam didn't look away, he stared right back at his uncle until Willie turned away to follow Iris up to the back door. Adam started to climb off the back of the truck.

"Adam! Stay here!" Aunt Connie snapped at him.

He hesitated for a moment and then jumped off the truck, watching Iris. She didn't knock, she just walked right in the back door with Willie at her heels. "What are you doing?" He heard Isaac shout. "Billie!" Adam heard Connie say. He turned around and Billie was also getting off the back of the truck. Adam quietly climbed the step and slipped into the house. The inside was almost as shabby as the outside.

"I want what's mine," he heard Iris say.

"What are you talking about?" Isaac said.

"Father sent me away with nothing."

"You defied him! You defied the will of God!" Isaac sputtered.

"What did he know about the will of God?" Iris raised her voice. "You're confusing the will of the Almighty with the will of an angry, selfish man."

Isaac's face turned red. "Get out!" he screamed.

Iris defiantly walked over to a small desk in the sitting room and started to rummage through the doors. Adam saw Samuel standing in the doorway in his nightshirt. He looked confused and frightened.

"Stop that!" Isaac screamed at Iris.

She looked at him and scowled. She lowered her voice but there was an iciness to it. "Just some money. Consider it the dowery father never had to pay Abram Schrock."

"There is no money!" Isaac protested.

Iris brushed past him into the cooking area. She started looking into a set of canisters and then stopped when she got to the smallest one. She reached in and took out a roll of bills. "The same place Poppa used to keep it," she added bitterly.

"Put that back! You have no right!" Isaac said taking a step towards her.

She glared at him. "You're just like him you know that? A stubborn, self-righteous old fool." She went to step around him but he grabbed her arm.

"He was right about you!" Isaac roared. "You have no morals. You are evil."

"Coming from him that's a compliment. I hope he's burning in Hell!" Iris went to pull away but Isaac tightened his grip and with his free hand slapped Iris hard across the face. Before anyone else could react, Willie was across the room in three steps and plunged his knife into Isaac's abdomen. A look of shock crossed Isaac's face. He grabbed at Willie's wrists but Willie just drove the knife deeper into Isaac and then forced it up into his chest. Isaac tumbled over backwards with Willie on top of him.

Adam stood frozen. It had happened again. Billie's screaming barely registered with him. Iris stood looking down at Willie rolling off of Isaac, covered in blood. Isaac lay on the floor, looking up at the ceiling with vacant eyes, the life oozing out of him. Iris' expression was a mix of emotions. Billie had stopped screaming and stood frozen also. Connie rushed in and covered her mouth with her hands.

Iris came out of her brief reverie. She pocketed the roll of bills and smoothed her dress. She looked away from her dying brother and said, "Let's go."

Adam thought about refusing or just running out of the house and running off in any direction, just to escape the insanity. He found that he couldn't move though.

"What about him?" Billie's voice cut in. She was pointing at Samuel who stood with a look of shock on his face.

Iris seemed to notice the boy for the first time. She

looked back at Billie. "What about him? Leave him."

"No!" Billie said. "He's just a little boy!"

Iris glared at her with her cool gray eyes. "He's not our problem," she said.

Billie pointed at Willie and yelled, "He made him our problem, didn't he?"

Iris walked up to Billie and slapped her. Billie's eyes filled with tears but she stared hard back at her grandmother.

"Billie Jean!" Connie's voice cut in. "You will not speak to your grandmother like that!"

Billie stuck her chin out and said, "I'm not leaving without him. Willie walked up and stood next to Iris. Billie pointed at him again and said. "He'll have to gut me and drag me out of here to get me to leave."

Adam shot Willie a quick, terrified glance. Willie was breathing hard and had a vacant look in his eyes. He was still holding the knife but in his blood covered hand but he gripped it loosely at his side. Through Adam's fear though he resolved at that moment that Willie would have to kill him first before he let him harm Billie. He looked at Iris, who for the first time in his memory seemed unsure of what to say or do. Billie must have seen that as an opening because she walked right past her, scooped Samuel up in her arms and carried him back to his room to get his things.

CHAPTER 26

B y the time Billie had returned a moment later with
Samuel and a pillowcase full of his belongings Iris
had regained her bearings.

"Let's go," she said sharply.

"But what about..." Connie started to say, pointing at
Isaac's body.

"There's no time," Iris said as she moved towards the
door.

Iris made Willie strip off his bloody shirt and throw it
into an abandoned well. As they climbed into the truck Adam
wonders how long it would be until someone found Isaac's body.
The man had lived more or less as a hermit the past few years.
He shuddered at the thought of the old man lying on the floor
of his run down house with no one to give him a proper burial.

It took most of the day to make the trip back to the
Hollow. No one said a word the whole way. Occasionally Adam
found himself gazing at Billie. She sat stoically holding Samuel
in her arms with a blanket wrapped around him. She looked
older somehow, like a full grown woman. Aunt Connie, on the
other hand, looked like she was in shock. She sat staring into

space with her hands worrying the hem of her skirt.

They arrived back at the Avery farm after six. Adam was sore and hungry. It occurred to him that they hadn't eaten all day. The family quietly disembarked from the truck. Billie was still holding Samuel so Adam picked up the pillow case.

"What are you going to do with him?" he asked.

"He can sleep in my room," Billie answered. She caught herself and looked at Adam. "Until your mother gets back.

Adam looked at her and nodded. Iris and Connie had already retired to their bedrooms by the time they got upstairs. Billie laid Samuel down on the bed. He stirred slightly and then began breathing deeply again.

"I guess we're on our own for supper," Billie said. "Are you hungry?"

"Starved," Adam replied.

"Let's go downstairs. I think there's a rabbit in the icebox and some potatoes in the pantry." Before they left Billie reached into the pillowcase and removed a dusty book.

"What's that?" Adam asked.

"It's a book on American Sign Language. I found it in Samuel's room"

Adam looked at the cover and said, "Looks like it hasn't been opened in a while."

The rabbit turned out to have gone bad so they made do with boiled potatoes and corn. After they ate Adam cleaned up while Billie went up to check on Samuel. Finding him still asleep she came back and helped Adam finish the dishes. Neither Iris nor Connie had emerged from their rooms or had Willie reappeared. It was starting to get dark and Adam was exhausted. He looked at Billie and she had dark circles under her eyes. Suddenly she looked back at him.

"What are we going to do?" she asked.

"I don't know," he said flatly. "But I don't think we can stay here."

"Where would we go?

"I don't know!" He snapped and immediately regretted his tone.

Billie looked taken aback. Adam felt his cheeks flush and then said, I'm sorry... I'll think of something. I'm just so tired."

Billie put a hand on his cheek. "We'll think of something," she said.

They said goodnight and Adam slunk off to the bunkhouse. The Shadows had taken over the musty room. There was no light on and no sign of Willie. He thought it would be hard to sleep with his mad uncle wandering around but as soon as he lay down on his cot fully clothed, he drifted off.

The dreams came again, fire, blood, blurred images of his parents' faces.

^^^

Daybreak. Adam opened his eyes. It took him a moment to differentiate between what he had been dreaming and what was real. His head was throbbing and he was covered in perspiration. He sat up. Willie had either never returned or he had crept in during the night or had left already. Something registered in his peripheral vision, something that had registered before he went to bed but with the fatigue and the failing light his mind had chosen to ignore it. He looked at his nightstand. His books were gone, the last worldly connection he had to a slightly happier time. Willie.

Who else could it have been? He was pretty sure Willie was functionally illiterate but that wouldn't have stopped him from taking the books out of pure spite.

He walked over to the foot locker that was at the foot of Willie's cot and threw it open. He rummaged through it and only found soiled and worn clothing. In the corner of the room was the locker where Willie kept his hunting rifles. He knew Willie kept the key with him at all times so he would have to find a way into it. He looked around the bunkhouse and saw nothing. He ran outside and found a fist-sized rock next to the path. Adam took the rock back inside and started to smash it into the locker handle. Again and again he brought the rock down onto the handle. He was fueled by anger and frustration, not worried that Willie could walk in at any moment.

He had no idea how long he beat on the handle or notice of his bleeding knuckles but after a while the handle bent downward and after a few more determined blows it came off. The locker didn't pop open as he had hoped so he stuck his finger in drawing blood again on the jagged metal. He worked his finger around until he found the latch mechanism and popped the door.

Willie's shotgun was missing but the .22 rabbit rifle was still there. He rummaged through the locker, no books. He was just about to slam it shut when a metallic glimmer caught his eye. There, hanging on a hook, was the pendant that Jacob had given Maureen as an engagement present.

Willie. He'd known in his heart that his mother would have never deserted him. Of course they had to silence her. Iris had always treated Maureen as an outsider and Willie was Iris' willing stooge. His vision flashed red. He took the locket and turned to leave. He stopped suddenly and turned back to the locker. He removed the .22, found a box of shells and loaded it.

He ran to the house and threw open the front door. No one in the parlor. He walked into the kitchen and came face to face with Connie and Iris. Connie looked at Adam and then the rifle and her mouth fell open. Iris stood looking at him expressionless.

"Where is he?" Adam hissed.

Connie stepped back, Iris crossed her arms in front of her and said, "What do you think you're doing?"

Adam raised the rifle and pointed it at Iris. "You knew, didn't you?"

Iris closed her eyes. "It was an accident," she said.

"I've witnessed Willie's accidents," Adam said.

"It was!" Iris exclaimed. "She brought it on herself! Your mother didn't understand... she never understood. I am fighting for this family's survival."

"Well you're doing a shit job. My parents are dead, you killed grandpa, Uncle John's run off."

Iris fumed, "How dare you?" The only reason you're still here is because of your late father. You and Billie don't understand the sacrifices I've made."

"Jacob wasn't his father!" Connie blurted out.

They both looked at her. She had turned pale and she was shaking. Adam swung the rifle in Connie's direction. She took a step back and almost fell over the table.

"What... what did you say?" Adam asked in disbelief.

Connie looked at Iris. "It's true!" She said. "Maureen was pregnant when she met Jacob!

"Shut your mouth!" Adam screamed.

Connie looked at Adam. "She told me herself," she said.

"You're a liar!"

"He's not family!" Connie said pointing at Adam. "Maureen got pregnant."

Adam had heard enough. He leveled the gun at Connie's head and his finger tightened around the trigger.

"Stop!" Iris screamed.

Adam's hands were shaking and his eyes were tearing up. Connie was frozen where she stood. Billie entered the kitchen with Samuel hiding behind her legs.

"Adam," Billie said softly. "What's going on?"

"They killed my ma," Adam said weakly.

Billie let that sink in. She looked at Iris and then shot her mother a withering look.

"You're not like them," she said to Adam.

Iris had inched over to the wash tub. While Billie had been speaking she had reached down next to the tub and pulled out Willie's shotgun. Before Adam knew what was happening he heard the *click* of one barrel being cocked. With the rifle still pointed in Connie's direction he glanced over at Iris.

"I don't know if you're my grandson or not, but I will shoot you if you don't put that gun down," Iris said. Instead Adam swung the gun in Iris' direction. Iris cocked the other barrel. "That's a Twenty-two. You'll put a hole in me true enough." She turned her aim to Billie and Samuel. "But I'll kill these two and that will be on your conscience."

Adam wavered. He raised the weapon at Iris again and watched her finger tighten around the trigger. He glanced at Billie, who was doing her best to shield Samuel and then lost his resolve. He lowered the rifle and set it on the floor at his feet.

"Connie, pick it up," Iris said. Connie didn't move. She was standing with a look of smug relief on her face. "Constance!" Iris barked. Connie snapped out of her funk, glanced at Iris and then cautiously walked over and picked up the rifle. As soon as she had it in her hands she scurried away from Adam and stood next to Iris.

Iris un-cocked the shotgun and lowered it. "You ungrateful..." she stated to say to Adam and Billie. She was interrupted by a knock on the front door. "Connie, go see who that is and get rid of them,"

Connie looked at her mother, a look of confusion on her

face and then down at the .22 she was holding like it was a live snake. "Give me that," Iris said. Connie handed her the rifle and then rushed out to the parlor. They heard the door open and then it was silent for a moment.

Finally a voice; "Constance... are your parents about?" Adam recognized the voice of Sheriff Ed Ferguson.

"Um... mom's in the kitchen..." Connie said with a slight waver in her voice.

Again a moment of silence and then Ferguson's voice, "Do you mind if we come in?"

Iris glared at Billie and Adam. She set the .22 down on the counter top and hissed, "Stay in here and don't say a word." She walked out into the parlor with the shotgun against her leg, obscured by the folds of her skirt. "What's this all about?" She asked loudly. Adam peeked his head into the parlor. Iris had stopped just behind Connie, using her to block the Sheriff's view of the gun.

Ferguson, still standing on the porch looked at Iris coolly. "Iris, we're looking for Silas. He hasn't been seen or heard from in two days."

"Well we haven't seen him." Iris replied. Adam could see another deputy through the window, standing just off the porch. He was heavyset with a full mustache, just like Ferguson.

Ferguson's look hardened. "He told Ida at the office that he was headed over this way..."

Iris interrupted, "And I said we haven't seen him!'"

Just then, footsteps, running up from the side of the house. Through the window Adam saw another deputy, a smooth faced young man, barely out of his teens. He was holding his hat in his hand and was red faced from exertion.

"Sheriff…" he puffed, out of breath. "Silas's car… it's here… a bunch of dead cows…"

It took a moment for Ferguson to register what the young deputy was saying. By the time he turned his head angrily to look back at Iris she had raised the shotgun and cocked one of the barrels. Connie screamed and jumped off to the side. Ferguson started to reach for the revolver on his hip but then the shotgun roared and he was blown backwards off the porch where he landed with a thud on his back. His chest was flecked with blood and his body jerked once then he lay still. The older deputy already had his weapon drawn and fired off two shots as Iris pushed the door closed. The bullets cracked into the wooden door and Connie shrieked.

Adam turned around and looked at Bille. He pointed at the back door and yelled, "Let's go." He shepherded Billie and Samuel out the door and looked back at the .22 on the counter. He thought about taking it but then realized he had no idea how many lawmen were outside. If they saw anyone of the murderous Averys with a weapon surely they would shoot them down. More gunshots behind them as they ran towards the barn.

"Can you drive the truck?" Adam asked Billie.

"Yes, I think so," she replied as she scooped up Samuel in her arms.

They were twenty yards from the barn when Adam saw Willie running from the other direction towards them. He was closing in fast but still thirty yards away. Willie had either heard the gunshots or known they were running, he had his knife drawn and was wild eyed.

Adam pushed the barn door open. "Up in the loft!" He yelled as Billie carried Samuel past him.

Billie threw Samuel over her shoulder and with surprising strength climbed the ladder to the loft. Adam was right behind them and looked over his shoulder just as Willie entered the barn and paused while his eyes adjusted to the shadows. Willie looked at Adam and with renewed hate in his eyes ran towards the ladder. Billie had made it to the top of the ladder. She paused to deposit Samuel onto the loft and then climbed up after him. Adam was one rung from the top when he felt Willie's hand grab his ankle. Willie pulled and it was all Adam could do to keep his grip. Willie grunted as he pulled again but Adam held firm. Just as Willie was getting ready to pull again Adam kicked down as hard as he could. The force broke Willie's grasp and Adam's shoe connected with Willie's face. Adam could feel the cartilage in Willie's nose snap and then Willie lost his grip and fell back to the ground. Adam climbed the rest of the way up into the loft. He rolled over onto his back and tried to catch his breath. He looked at Billie who was cradling Samuel in her arms. The boy's face was expressionless and his eyes blank. It was quiet down below, too quiet. Adam peeked over the edge of the loft and saw that Willie, with blood streaming out of his nose, ascending the ladder with the knife in his teeth, like Tarzan in the pictures.

Adam frantically looked around the loft. There, leaning against a post was an old rusty pitchfork. He ran over to grab it as Willie topped the ladder. Willie had the knife in his hand and took a step towards Adam.

"I'm goin' to gut you boy!" Willie said.

"Is that what you did to my ma?"

Willie looked wounded. He shook his head. "That was an accident. She was supposed to marry me!" His voice was on odd combination of anger and sorrow.

Adam raised the pitchfork. "She would have never married you!" he screamed.

"Jacob was dead! She needed a husband!"

"Not you!" Adam spat. "She felt sorry for you. She was too good a person to hate you like everyone else does..."

"Shut your mouth!" Willie growled. "Nothing would have happened if she hadn't blabbed to Silas. Ma told me to tell her to be quiet but she started screaming and..." Willie stopped. The memory of what had happened between Maureen and himself too raw to put into words.

"You son of a bitch!" Adam said. He lunged at Willie with the pitchfork but Willie deftly sidestepped him and pushed him as he went by. Adam hadn't realized how close he had been to the edge until the floor disappeared beneath him. He felt momentarily weightless as he fell. His left foot hit the hard ground first and his knee twisted and he felt a pop. He fell onto his side and his left elbow hit the ground hard. A sharp pain suddenly stabbed at his knee. He rolled onto his back and saw Willie looking down at him smiling.

"Iris is dead," he heard Billie say.

Willie swung around to her. "What?" he said.

"We just came from the house. Those gunshots you heard? She shot Sheriff Ferguson and then the deputies shot her."

"You're lying," Willie said turning in her direction.

"It's true," Billie continued. "They were looking for you 'cause they know what you've done."

Willie looked lost for a moment and then looked down at Adam, sitting up now, holding his knee.

"Sheriff was saying that if they didn't give you the electric chair they were going to put you in an asylum. Iris didn't like that," Billie said.

Willie glared at her. "What are you going to do now that there's no one to order you around?" Billie said.

"Nobody orders me around."

Billie laughed bitterly. "No one to tell you when to get up. What to eat. When to wipe your ass."

"This is all your fault!" Willie screamed at Billie. "You and Adam! Everything was fine until you all showed up."

"Fine like how Leon used to beat you for being an idiot?" Billie teased.

Willie's face was contorted with rage. He moved towards Billie. Adam couldn't see them now but he could tell by

the dust and hay falling through the floorboards of the loft that
Billie was backing away towards the far end of the barn. He
painfully got to his feat and with the excruciating pain in his
knee hobbled after them from below, using the pitchfork as a
crutch

"Aren't you in enough trouble?" Billie said. The teasing
tone had been replaced by fear.

"All your fault!" Willie repeated.

They were nearing the back of the barn. There was a
small pile of moldy hay on the floor. "Billie!" Adam yelled.

She looked over the edge. "Jump!" Adam screamed.

A brief look of doubt crossed her face. One glance
back in Willie's direction was enough to convince her though.
She tightened her arms around Samuel and jumped. She hit the
hay feet first and then rolled onto her back. She grimaced in
pain and sat up. There was small piece of broken glass sticking out of her back. Her main focus was still on Samuel. She
looked into his face. He was crying now but seemed otherwise
uninjured.

Adam helped her up. "Run!" he said.

She stepped out of the hay and started running towards
the door. Adam looked up and right into Willie's eyes. Willie
looked back towards the ladder at the other end of the loft and
then seemed to reconsider. He got ready to jump. Adam took
a step back as if he was going to make a break for it too but
as Willie jumped he stepped back towards the pile of hay and
brought the pitchfork up.

Willie barely had time to register what was happening. Adam tried to brace himself as Willie crashed into the pitchfork. The collision knocked Adam to the ground, a fresh wave of pain exploding in his knee. His eyes filled and then his vision blurred. He waited for the blade of Willie's knife to plunge into his exposed back but it didn't come. He rolled over and sat up slowly.

Willie was laying in the hay, the pitchfork handle had broken, but the fork had entered Willie's neck and chin at an upward angle. He was making a guttural gurgling noise and blood was pouring out of his mouth. Adam laid down again and closed his eyes.

"We have to go," Billie's voice came to him.

Adam opened his eyes. Billie was standing over him with her hand out. "Samuel's in the truck. We need to leave." She helped him to his feet   she supported him over to the passenger side door and then helped him in.

She accelerated out of the barn and had a good head of speed going as they passed the house. The younger deputy was struggling with Connie, trying to get her into the squad car. The older deputy was tending to the Sheriff. He looked up when he saw the truck speed by towards the road.

"Who was that? The older deputy yelled.

"It looked like the kids." The younger man replied still wrestling with an uncooperative Connie. "I didn't see Willie, but he might have been hiding in the back."

"Never mind them, we need to get the Sheriff to a doctor!"

Adam held Samuel on his lap as they drove past the scene at the front of the house, Sheriff Ferguson laying on the ground with the older deputy kneeling over him, the younger deputy struggling with a distraught Connie. There was no sign of Iris but then he noticed there was smoke pouring out of the front door. His knee was throbbing and he was covered with dirt and perspiration.

"Turn right out of the driveway and head north," he said to Billie as he wiped his eyes.

CHAPTER 27

April 1944

Mickey Burke had run worse cons. He was currently traveling around rural New York State selling jugs of water dyed and mixed with fertilizer to a bunch of hayseed farmers as a proclaimed "Miracle Grower" The trace amounts of fertilizer gave the stuff the stench of shit that these bumpkins seemed to actually enjoy.

His last scam had landed him in the jackpot, selling fake war bonds that his buddy Maury had made up after hours at his print shop. Somebody had squawked to the cops and he had to leave Brooklyn in the middle of the night. Maury wasn't so lucky. He got pinched and was looking at a long stretch in a Federal pen.

He had twelve gallon jugs of his "Farmer's Friend" miracle fertilizer in the back of the Packard. It wasn't going to make him rich, but it would keep him afloat until he found something better. As he drove along the country road he looked down at himself. The cuffs on his suit were starting to fray and his shoes were scuffed. He'd need to address his wardrobe as soon as he was flush.

It was getting late. He'd hoped to unload a few more gallons of the stuff before it got dark and he'd have to pull off the road and sleep in the car again. God knew where you could find a cheap hotel out in this backwater. He'd been told by another grifter, a guy he met in Olean selling bogus life insurance policies, that there were some likely marks up in Zoar Valley. Some genuine ignoramuses. He found himself on a tree lined road though that seemed to be going nowhere. He was thinking about turning around and making his way back to the main road when he saw a mailbox next to a gravel driveway. He pulled up closer. It was a new simple white wooden box with the name *Spencer* hand painted in neat, block lettering. Burke put the car back into gear and turned up the drive.

The trees thinned and he came up to a modest house. It looked freshly painted and there were flower pots on the porch. Off to the side two men were looking under the hood of an ancient, rusted pickup. The men looked up when they heard his tires on the gravel. The taller one was younger, blond and handsome. The second man's age was harder to determine, he may have been in his twenties, but there was a wariness about him that made him seem older. Burke straightened his tie and popped out of the car.

"Good evening gentlemen," he said cheerily as he tipped his fedora.

"Evening," the older man said. The blond man said nothing, he just stared at Burke expressionless.

"Having some trouble there?" Burke said pointing at

the truck.

The older man wiped his hands on a dirty rag. "Yep," he nodded. "I'm afraid the old girl's about had it." He looked at Burke then. "Can I help you with something?"

Burke removed his hat and said, "Oh I do apologize sir. My name is Michael Burns and I represent the Farmer's Friend Fertilizer Company out of White Plains." He offered his hand to the man.

The older man held up his hand despite his best effort with the rag it was still covered with grease. "No offense," he said. "I'm Adam Spencer and this is my son Sam."

Burke pulled his hand back and chuckled. "None taken Mr. Spencer. And I understand the busy life of a hard working farmer like yourself so I'll get right to it. I happen to have the very latest in fertilizer technology in the car with me. We've been fanning out all over the area to offer some introductory samples to fine, hardworking people just like yourself, backbone of the war effort if I do say so myself."

"You don't say?"

"Ha ha, I do say. It's concentrated so a few gallons will cover about ten acres. Are you getting ready to plant?"

Adam shook his head. "We grow mostly potatoes here. Planted after the last frost in March."

"Well Mr. Spencer, the beauty of Farmer's Friend is you can apply it at any time during the growing season. The nutrients in it help your plants grow and protect them from blight."

"Hmm," Adam nodded. "That is interesting." He threw

the rag onto the fender of the truck and stepped forward with a pronounced limp on his left side.

Burke noticed the limp and asked, "War wound?"

"No, had an accident when I was a boy. Never did heal right."

"What about your son? Is he draft age?"

Adam looked at Burke. "Not yet. Doesn't matter anyway. He's been deaf since birth."

Something in Adam's expression made Burke uneasy. "That's a shame..." he started. "I was 4F myself, flat feet."

Adam looked past Burke at the Packard. "Nice car. Had it long?"

Burke looked at Adam quizzically. "Um... no, it's a company car." It was in fact stolen from a neighbor back in the city.

Adam turned and looked at Sam. "Go tell your ma we have company," he said loudly and slowly. Sam dutifully trotted off to the house.

"Oh, I don't want to put you or the missus out," Burke said.

"Don't worry about it!" Adam exclaimed slapping Burke on the shoulder. "It's getting a little chilly out here. Why don't you come in and tell me more about this Farmer's Friend over a glass of homemade mash? I think you might even make a sale."

Burke grinned and said, "I suppose a short one wouldn't hurt."

Adam smiled. "It's my grandmother's secret recipe.

It'll fix you up right." And with the sun setting behind the trees Adam led Mickey Burke into the house.

EPILOGUE

It had taken hours but Billie and Adam found their way to Spencer's farm. Adam explained what had happened at the Spencer brother's and how Spencer had told him they were welcome to come back stay as long as they wanted to. It only took a few months before Tom Spencer told them that they were like "The children we never had," and they had a home there as long as they wanted.

A few years passed and Jesse Spencer succumbed to his myriad health problems. Billie had taught Samuel sign language and he was emerging as a bright, well-mannered boy. Tom Spencer and Adam worked side by side in the fields and they developed a bond that could only be broken by Tom's passing in '39. He left the farm to Adam and Billie.

Adam loved Billie more than any man could love a woman, though they never lay together as man and wife. Even with Connie's claim that Jacob wasn't his real father he would always think of Billie as his blood. They raised Samuel as their own son. When he was eighteen they enrolled him at the Pennsylvania School for the Deaf. They hated the thought of him not being with them every day but he was bright and imaginative. They wanted him to experience more of the world than a potato farm in Zoar Valley.

The dreams Adam had about fire and blood came less frequently. He would wonder from time to time what had happened to Iris. Had she been shot down? Burned in the fire? Or was there a remote chance that she had escaped? He never would know. But he did know that whatever had happened to Iris, she, or anyone else for that matter, would never take advantage of himself or his loved ones again.

About the Author

David Coleman is a native of Buffalo, new York. He curently lives in Hamburg, New York with his wife and two daughters. For more information on David's writing please visit rustbeltwriter.com.

Acknowledgments

To my home based "focus group;" my wife Jeanne and daughters Emily and Liz. Also my friend and editor Cynthia Lehman for her efforts, constructive criticism and support. To my parents who taught me the value of books. And to all the people who read and gave such positive feedback on the Donovan series.